ANATOMIES

ALSO BY ANNDEE HOCHMAN

Everyday Acts & Small Subversions:
Women Reinventing Family, Community and Home

Anndee Hochman

PICADOR USA
NEW YORK

for Elissa
all this, and more

ANATOMIES

A NOVELLA AND STORIES

www.picadorusa.com

Picador® is a U.S. registered trademark and is used by St. Martin's Press under license from Pan Books Limited.

For information on Picador USA Reading Group Guides, as well as ordering, please contact the Trade Marketing department at St. Martin's Press.
Phone: 1-800-221-7945 extension 763
Fax: 212-677-7456
E-mail: trademarketing@stmartins.com

Some of the stories in this book were originally published in the following:

"Liability" (an earlier version), in *Evergreen Chronicles* (Minneapolis), Summer 1999.
"Aggiornamento," in *Women's Words* (Maynard, Massachusetts), Winter/Spring 1999.
"In Case of Emergency," in *Love Shook My Heart: New Lesbian Love Stories,* edited by Irene Zahava (Los Angeles: Alyson Publications, 1998). First published in *Boston Review* (Boston), April 1997.
"Local Currency" (previously titled "Nothing Matters More Than This"), in *International Quarterly* (Tallahassee), December 1998.
"Diamonds Are a Girl's Best Friend," in *The Seven Hills Fiction Review* (Tallahassee), Winter 1997.
"Nesting," in *Talus & Scree #3: An International Literary Journal* (Waldport, Oregon), October 1997. First published in *The Toronto Star,* June 13, 1994.
"Anatomies," in *City Paper* (Philadelphia), December 31, 1993.
"Dark Is Not a Single Shade of Gray," in *Glimmer Train Stories* (Portland, Oregon), Winter 1991.

Excerpt from "Jerusalem" copyright © 1994 by Naomi Shihab Nye. Reprinted from *Red Suitcase,* by Naomi Shihab Nye, with the permission of BOA Editions, Ltd.

Book designed by Michelle McMillian

Library of Congress Cataloging-in-Publication Data

Hochman, Anndee.
    Anatomies / Anndee Hochman
       p. cm.
    ISBN 0-312-24118-6 (hc)
    ISBN 0-312-27005-4 (pbk)
    1. United States—Social life and customs—20th century—Fiction. I. Title

PS3558.O339 A83 2000
813'.54—dc21   00-027324

First Picador USA Paperback Edition: August 2001

10 9 8 7 6 5 4 3 2 1

Acknowledgments

The storyteller speaks in her own voice, but the source of her telling is a shared tapestry of experience and imagination. My appreciation extends to all the people who helped me locate, name, and shape these stories.

I have been privileged to work with teachers who gave generously of themselves while expecting excellence: Judith Barrington, Andrea Carlisle, Evelyn C. White, and the late John Hersey. The Leeway Foundation, the Astraea National Lesbian Action Foundation, and the Pennsylvania Council on the Arts provided grants that, for a fiction writer, translated to the sweet gift of time. From the incomparable women of the 29th Street Writers—Karen Brummel-Smith, Elissa Goldberg, Kathleen Haley, Cherry Hartman, Mary Henning-Stout, Kathleen Herron, Janet Howey, Shirley Kishiyama, Mimi Maduro, Amy Schutzer, and Ila Suzanne—I received essential critique, powerful example, and sisterly love.

My agent, the most excellent Amy Rennert, cared for these

stories from the beginning and shepherded them into the world with grace and persistence. I am grateful to George Witte, my editor, for reading thoughtfully between the lines and asking questions that helped to enlarge the work.

I wish to thank my family, particularly my parents, Gloria and Stan Hochman, for telling stories—and listening to mine—with such unflagging delight and boundless love. My friends on both coasts (and in-between) help make my world a rich and fabulous place to live and consistently remind me what it means to be a human being. And a deep heartbeat of gratitude and love goes to Elissa Goldberg, my partner, who heard every word.

Each carries a tender spot:
something our lives forgot to give us.

—NAOMI SHIHAB NYE

Contents

Contents

NERVE

FLESH

In Case of Emergency

We buried Hank's umbilical stump in the backyard, in sight of the basketball hoop, spitting distance from where the cucumbers will be. Emmy donated the box from her first pair of real earrings, and we nestled the stump on the little mattress of cotton. It was about as big as my thumb.

Hank's mother, Della, who was certifiably nuts but had moments of stunning lucidity, sent us the remains of Hank's umbilical after her last visit. His dementia was pretty advanced by then, and Hank kept calling her "Morning Glory," which was his own drag name—but we didn't tell her that.

Two days after Della got on the bus for Newark, a small envelope arrived Federal Express. Inside was a Ziploc bag and, inside that, the dessicated leftover of the cord that, thirty-four years earlier, had looped Della and Hank together in a perfect ecosystem. Obviously, Della was cutting her ties, shedding the apron strings and the apron, too. That package said, "He's your responsibility now." As if we didn't know.

At first, I thought it was a piece of dried-up cat poop. But Mo, who'd worked in a women's health clinic, recognized the withered, rust brown bit for what it was. "Gross," Emmy said when we told her. "I hope you two didn't save mine." We hadn't, actually—even though placenta rituals were coming back in vogue when we gave birth to Em. Some of our friends even cooked theirs into soup. That sounded revolting, so we'd wrapped ours in the Sunday comics and buried it in the yard.

It was getting crowded out there. Already underground were Moishe the hamster, Hemingway the parrot, Nora the goldfish, a stray cat that died before we'd had time to name her, and Mo's diaphragm, which she'd given a ritualistic burial to mark her coming-out years ago. It was an ethical dilemma at the time, diaphragms not being biodegradable, but Mo finally justified the burial by thinking of all the condoms, spermicide tubes, and K-Y she'd have used if she'd stayed straight. Surely her diaphragm was a lesser contribution to the nation's landfill.

Hank wanted to be buried in the yard, too—"I need to apologize to Moishe for saying his tail was ugly," he said—but it turned out the county had laws about the disposal of bodies on private property, and it's hard to find the chutzpah for civil disobedience when you can't stop crying. So we had him cremated and threw the ashes off Steel Pier in Atlantic City, which was his second choice. The gray crumbs floated for a moment; then a wave came in like a giant claw and snatched Hank into the undertow.

On the way back from the shore, we told stories. How Hank loved the sound of words and would pronounce his favorites— *unctuous, serendipity, calcification*—again and again, until they sounded like gibberish. How he knew things—the difference between braising and sautéing, how to knit a sock, what molly bolts were for. How he'd come over to tune our piano one August and just stayed.

Hank was a friend of a friend of Mo's, and he'd been camping on various sofa beds ever since his lover died. We invited him for dinner and breakfast and dinner again, until we stopped counting and just set the table for four every time. Afterward, Hank would do the dishes, soap bubbles gloving his wiry forearms, hair flaming in the kitchen's caramel light.

Hank collected trivia, but he never made you feel stupid for not knowing. He told us the slang for *gay* and *lesbian* in a dozen languages. The only ones I remember are *faygeleh* in Yiddish and *malas flores*, Spanish for "bad flowers." Hank knew the names of the Indian tribes who lived here before, and he was the one who told us that Poe's raven, the actual bird, was stuffed and preserved and stood on a closet shelf at the central branch of Philadelphia's Free Library. All you had to do was ask.

That trip to the library was his last one out of the house. All the way there in the car, Hank and Emmy recited "The Raven" and "Annabel Lee" and any other Poe they could remember. Em's favorite line, naturally, was "Nevermore," which she'd begun using in answer to routine questions from Mo and me: "Emmy, would you like some string beans?" "*Nevermore.*" "Em, how about practicing the piano?" "*Nevermore!*"

The two of them were giddy with adrenaline and springtime, so Mo and I pretended not to notice that Hank felt like a cheap marionette—all balsa wood and paper clip hinges—when we lifted him from the backseat into the wheelchair. Emmy skipped along beside him, singing lines from Poe, until we got to the library closet where the raven was kept. As soon as the librarian opened the door and a smell of old bones floated out, I saw

Hank's hand grip the arm of his chair. The bird's feathers were the tired black of ruined suede gloves, its eyes flat and opaque. It listed to one side as though it would rather lie down.

"Close it," Hank said to the librarian, and when her hand paused a minute on the knob, he said it again. "I mean it. Close the goddamned door." Emmy began to cry. We drove home in silence.

Even after that, Hank still had the energy for our postdinner games of Clue, all four of us crowded on his bed. He always took Miss Scarlett, of course, and made absurd guesses, full of political and artistic allusion. "Colonel North with an Uzi in the Persian Gulf room," he'd say, or "Van Gogh with a paintbrush in the atelier."

"What's an atelier?" Emmy asked, and Hank explained that van Gogh had made himself crazy in his studio from eating lead-based paint.

"Why?" Em said, and even Hank did not have an answer to that. "Why?" she said again, and greeted our silence with an impatient toss of her hair. At ten, she was just discovering the depths of what grown-ups do not understand. We failed her daily, but so far she had managed to forgive our astonishing ignorance.

"Mom, could Hank be my dad?" she asked once, shortly after he started to live with us. Mo and I exchanged the "Okay, here goes" look. We were all set to explain about sperm donors and insemination clinics and moms who *really want a baby*, but then Mo said, "How come, sweetie?"

"I mean, I know he's our friend and our housemate and everything, but there's a father-daughter basketball dinner, and I thought maybe he could just pretend."

As it turned out, Hank got sick and couldn't go, so Mo escorted

Emmy to the dinner. She even wore a dress. There was a gay father who spotted Mo's drag right away, and the two of them had a great time talking. Emmy got an award for Player with the Best Vocabulary. I stayed home and blotted night sweats with a Mickey Mouse beach towel.

That was last spring, a year ago. Now we are burying Hank's umbilical stump and saying what we will remember most.

"His hot-and-sour soup," said Mo, who falls asleep at night reading back issues of *Food & Wine*.

"The sound of his voice," I said.

Em shifted from one foot to the other. "What he told me about dying," she said finally. "He told me it hurt, and that he didn't believe any of that stuff about white light and angels, but he wouldn't mind hanging out with other dead people, because they were some of the most interesting. Except for us, that is."

She bent down and put the white box in the hole I'd dug. Mo troweled dirt over it, then wiped her face with a brown hand.

"Bye, Hank," Em said. "Nevermore."

"Never more," I said. "Never enough."

In the fall, when the ground is gray and the sun sets early, we will plant bulbs in the place where Hank's umbilical cord is buried. We will choose sultry yellow irises and black-purple tulips, crazed fiery mums and lilies that arch open without the slightest hint of prudishness. Hank's cord will turn to mineral dust and mix with the remains of Moishe and Hemingway and the nameless cat, and everyone will forgive everyone. We'll weep daily into the garden. By next spring, our yard will be a ruckus of brave blooms, roots tangling underground, a whole field of *malas flores*.

What's More

When my mother was eight years old, she could not stop tying her shoes. She had those brown oxfords all kids wore back then, the kind of shoes that were easy to sell to immigrant parents who put clothing in the same category as medicine, not fashion. Those shoes were the footwear equivalent of cod-liver oil.

My mother woke up every morning on Dauphin Street, got dressed, gathered her books, and tied her shoes. Then she crouched down and retied them. The loops were uneven. She tied them again. The double knot looked messy. Again. The left one was too tight, the right too loose. Again.

"Ruchela, go already to school. Stop with the tying." My grandmother would give her a little push. My mother ran for the bus. Once she was on it, she drew her knees up under the hem of her dress, propped a book on the easel her legs made, heels of her oxfords resting on the green vinyl seat, and retied her shoes all the way down Cumberland Avenue to PS 34.

I heard this story for the first time just last week, when I came home for Thanksgiving. Everyone was there, and the room felt fetid and restless as a stable. As usual, my father got elected to carve the turkey because he is a scientist and the relatives think he should be good at dissecting things. My mother is a scientist, too, but as far as her family is concerned, she's just another second-generation daughter in an apron, pulling pans of stuffing out of the oven and forgetting to sit down.

Aunt Ceil passed me a bowl of sweet potatoes. "Do you want a little of this, dear?" I dumped a big spoonful onto my plate, which was already mounded with stuffing, scalloped white potatoes, and spears of celery from the relish tray.

"Oh," Ceil said, "Looks like you still have a healthy appetite. What do they feed you up there at college? A lot of starches, I bet."

"It's so hard to eat right in the dorms," my cousin Sarah said. "Everything's got gravy, and even the salad bar—do you know how many calories are in a cup of chickpeas?"

"Calories, shmalories." That was Sarah's mother, Bev. "I always say it doesn't matter what you eat as long as you burn it off. Are you still swimming, sweetheart?"

I shook my head. I'd gone up to the gym once, a few weeks into the semester. After a couple laps of breaststroke, the lifeguard tapped my shoulder and suggested I move from the "medium" to the "slow" lane, where I had to swim around a woman in a flowered cap who was jogging languidly through the water. Still, it was beautiful in the pool, buoyant and thickly silent. I imagined that each stroke magically thinned me, that when I got out, I'd be lithe as a seal. I imagined buying a stretchy red minidress and having the salesclerk wink conspiratorially when I modeled it in the three-way mirror. It would fit snugly as a sock, and I would look gorgeous.

When I got out of the pool, breathless after half a mile, eyes burning from chlorine and nearsighted to begin with, I practically stepped on my Humanities 104 teacher. He was wearing a tiny Speedo swimsuit, striped blue-and-white. I tried not to squint at it.

"Well, hello, Olivia," he said. "I've been meaning to talk to you. Are you enjoying the class?"

"Yeah."

"Are you having any problems with the reading?"

"No."

"Well, you're awfully quiet in class. I'd like to hear from you more often."

"Okay."

We were doing Aristotle, from a book that cost thirty-seven dollars and had pages thin as tissue, and I fell asleep after practically every paragraph. Once my roommate, Andrea, nudged me awake in the library. "Everyone's looking at you. Why don't you just go home and take a nap?" she hissed.

I swiped at a thread of drool. "No. Gotta stay up. Gotta finish the chapter." Andrea shrugged and flipped her red hair over one shoulder. She was a gymnast and a French major, from Albuquerque. Each morning, she swung her legs over the side of the top bunk before hopping down, and I watched her amber calves, the muscles tensed and ready, her feet swaying back and forth like metronomes.

Turkey?" Uncle Leo asked.

"No, thanks. I'm a vegetarian, remember?"

"I thought vegetarians were supposed to be skinny. All that rabbit food, right? Well, you don't know what you're missing."

I started to eat. The sweet potatoes had small sticky lozenges of brown sugar melting inside them. I ate slowly, the way I always have, keeping the different foods separate on my plate. When I was little, I ate counterclockwise, starting with the hour that matched my age—eight o'clock when I was eight, and so on. It stopped working when I was a teenager. Still, I liked those paper plates with separate compartments, so the foods didn't mix. I alternated colors: a bite of string beans with slivered almonds, a bite of stuffing, a piece of a roll puffy as cumulous clouds. For dessert, there was cousin Sylvia's famous fruit salad, two kinds of chocolate cake, and a tin of those imported butter cookies.

"Are you sure you want those?" my father asked when I pulled three of them from the top layer of fluted paper cups.

"Yes," I said, and he shrugged.

"Oh, Mordy, she's a growing girl, leave her alone," Bev said.

My father hated for people to call him Mordy. It reminded him too much of Flatbush. His name was Martin, Mordechai in Hebrew. At work, they all called one another by their last names, even he and my mother. It's a good thing she'd kept her maiden name; otherwise, there would be two Berkowitzes answering every time some intern called across the room.

I was disappointed the first time I went to their lab. I thought it would be hushed, like a synagogue or church. Instead, there was a Bob Marley tape playing on a paint-spattered boom box and not a single person in a white coat. They were just a regular bunch of grown-ups getting excited about invisible stuff, calling each other Jenkins and McFarland, as if they were at soccer practice.

My parents had worked together at the university lab for years,

11

studying isotopes. My father was tall and thin; my mother was short and thin. Every morning, they ate cottage cheese on whole-grain bread and drank Lemon Zinger tea while reading the *New York Times*. Their idea of a great evening was to work in the garden until it got too dark to see, then eat tuna sandwiches while watching something on PBS with insects magnified to the size of your face. On weekends, they wore blue jeans with holes in the knees and each other's sweat socks. They were companionable as puppies.

I have a picture from the day they drove me up to college, the three of us posing in front of the Gothic window of my dorm. I'm wearing my usual army pants, and my thighs look like khaki-covered hams. My parents look proud and sad. I look worried and impatient. If the three of us had gone to college at the same time, I think, we would never have been friends.

Anyway, it was after dessert that night when I first heard the story of my mother and her shoe tying. I was sitting on the floor playing pat-a-cake with my littlest cousin, Max, when Aunt Millie spotted my shoes. They're nothing special, just a pair of knockoff Doc Martens I picked up at the Goodwill store.

"Rebecca, look at Livvie's shoes," she squealed. "Don't they look just like the ones you had, when you did that tying thing?"

"What tying thing?" I asked.

My mother laughed. "I've never told you? I had what we would now call an obsessive-compulsive disorder. I was still in elementary school. I just tied my shoes over and over. I couldn't help myself. Tanta Zena thought I was possessed. God, Millie, I haven't thought about that in years." She reached forward and pinched a pineapple chunk out of the fruit salad. "Okay, who needs another little sliver of cake?"

In retrospect, I don't know why I expected my parents' lab to feel holy, because they were the most determined atheists I'd ever met. They'd raised me and my brother, Mark, with a kind of channel-surfing approach to religion: five minutes on each topic, no commitment whatsoever. We'd gone to Christmas Eve candlelight services at Christ Church and dharma talks at a Zen center near Santa Fe. When we fasted and went to shul on Yom Kippur, it was like we were visiting the Smithsonian, ancient history that had nothing to do with our actual lives.

I remember sitting in the sanctuary at Temple Beth Torah, lulled nearly into a hypnotic trance from lack of food and the rabbi's chanting, paging through the prayer book, looking for the words that would unlock the mystery of why we were there, why we were Jewish and not Buddhist or Mormon or Episcopalian. I never found them. After the service, my parents would give each other a satisfied little glance, as if they'd just made sure Mark and I had had our five daily servings of fruits and vegetables.

"Gravity doesn't require that you believe in it," my dad used to say when I asked him why we weren't more observant. "It just keeps you attached to the earth. What more religion do you need?"

My mother had a little more to say on the subject. "There are beautiful stories in the Torah, Livvie, and some of the rituals are lovely. But I just found it all kind of . . . I don't know, limiting. After I left home, I just never felt the need for Shabbat candles and all the rest."

13

That's because you had your whole life figured out by the time you were twelve, I thought. My mother knew she wanted to be a scientist when she was in grade school. She met my father in their sophomore year at college, but they waited until after graduation to get married. Then they waited five more years to have me. Mark might have been an accident; they seemed surprised by him, even now. It was as if I'd been their project—the have-a-child hypothesis—and once their curiosity was satisfied, it was time to move on to other, more fascinating mysteries of the universe. Fortunately, Mark was a very low-maintenance kid who didn't require more than regular infusions of pizza and a high-quality stereo system.

After dinner that night, he and I sat in my old room, looking at the bulletin board filled with my high school art projects, still lifes of eggs and blocks, gritty charcoal shading on rough paper. Mark called it "the Livvie shrine" and said our parents were still hoping I'd move home after college.

"Fat chance," I said, instantly regretting my choice of words. But Mark never teased me about being chunky, even though he was built like my parents, chopstick-thin without trying. They worried about him because he got C's in English. But Mark knew he was smart; he had other plans. He was going to be a brilliant drummer, and he practiced for hours when he was supposed to be reading *Lord of the Flies*.

"Hey, you want these?" Mark dug into his backpack and pulled out a package of Archway cookies, chocolate walnut chip.

"Really?" I said. "You don't?"

"Nah, Tom brought them over this afternoon, but I don't really like that kind. You can take 'em back to school—you know, have a little party with your roommate."

"Thanks."

"Hey, Livvie?"

"Yeah?"

"It's kind of weird here when you're at college. I always feel sort of extra, like Mom and Dad are trying to have a meeting and I'm in the way. You know? On the other hand, there's not a million little bottles of pink stuff around the sink." Then he punched me in the arm on his way out of the room. Not a real punch, what our parents used to call a "potch." It meant, I love you, and you drive me crazy.

I opened the Archway cookies and smelled them. Oats and chocolate, toasted nuts and sugar. They were big cookies, three stacks of four each, the size of coasters. I could eat one from each stack, then rewrap them so it would look like they hadn't been touched. Or I could eat one whole stack and say Mark and I had shared them.

The first two were gone before I could even taste them. Okay, Livvie, slow down, I told myself. I chewed the third cookie carefully, feeling the pieces break apart in my teeth, my spit melting them from jigsaw edges to sweet mealy mouthfuls, the chocolate chips surrendering on my tongue. It was over too fast, and I wasn't full yet.

If I ate one more, it would be the last cookie—okay, the last dessert of any kind—until New Year's Eve. Between then and now, especially if I started swimming again, I could probably lose ten pounds. I'd invite my high school friends to a dinner party when we were home on break and knock them out by wearing a black velvet sheath dress, cut out in a V nearly to the butt in back, a low neckline that would show knobby collarbones. I'd act like it was nothing: Oh, that dorm food is so gross, who can eat it? I would make a brilliant observation about Aristotle, and Susie, the class valedictorian, would say she'd never thought about it that way. My parents would let us have wine, even though we were underage, as long as everyone promised not to drive home until we were sober. Then they'd go upstairs to watch *Koyaanisqatsi* for the seventh time. My friends would say good night, calling my parents by their first names.

I was on cookie number six. I'd eaten all of one stack, plus one each from the other two. My stomach was starting to churn, but I knew I wouldn't throw up. Even when I had stomach flu, I'd rather lie in bed, sweaty and shaking from nausea, than endure the short-term humiliation and relief of hanging my head over the toilet bowl.

I could hear my parents getting ready for bed: drawers closing, the *bip-bip-bip* as my father set the alarm. He had to leave early for a conference, so I probably wouldn't see him in the morning.

I was going back to school early to finish an incomplete. The libraries stayed open Thanksgiving weekend, on limited hours, and I knew who would be there: pale, fervent classics majors who ate all their meals from vending machines; a senior with designer glasses, hunched over the opera she just happened to be writing; and diffident prep school kids who couldn't go home because mummy and daddy were in Bologna on business. And me.

In high school, my friends and I prided ourselves on ducking labels: not trendies or jocks or dweebs. We dressed like the druggies but weren't as self-destructive; secretly, we cared about our grades a lot and wanted to get into good colleges so we could

16

leave home. On campus, I kept looking for the ones like that, the ones like me, but instead, I found beautiful Andrea, the only woman I'd ever known who actually went out on dates. There was the woman in my English class with the streak of magenta hair who'd already read the *Iliad* in Greek, and the guy downstairs, the architecture major who wore sandals all winter and who kept asking if I wanted to get high with him. I didn't.

So I spent a lot of time watching. I knew where the lesbians sat at the library, brazen on the couches in front of the huge plate-glass windows, sitting on one another's laps while they read Derrida and quantum physics. I knew which bathroom the bulimic girls used, the one with a water fountain inside it and indoor-outdoor carpet, not tile, on the floor. I knew which dorms to avoid walking past alone at night because the guys barfed out windows and tossed flaming wads of toilet paper into the courtyard when they were too drunk to know the difference.

Some nights, I got a big box of Milk Duds at the twenty-four-hour market and walked around the quad, chewing them slowly, looking up at the lighted lead-framed glass, yellow diamonds, the muffled shouts and shadows, ribbons of music and laughter, my heels ticking on the slate walkways, my teeth sticky with caramel. One time, I forgot my gate key and ended up sleeping on a couch in a little room outside the dining hall. When a maid came in to clean at 6:00 A.M., I jumped awake, and we both started apologizing.

"Oh, so sorry you scared. You sleeping. I not expect anyone."

"It's okay, I'm sorry, I was just—" I put on my sneakers and left her with her roaring vacuum. The streets felt mildewed. I walked myself to the nearest neon sign and ordered the greasy $2.99

farmer's breakfast, with a double order of hash browns to substitute for the sausage links. I was the only one at the counter.

Cookie number nine. Okay, I thought, enough, Livvie. If I want more tomorrow, they'll still be here. Or I could save them for the train ride back. Eat them while I read *The Death and Life of Great American Cities*. My blood felt crystallized, as if there were an IV drip of sugar flowing directly into my vein. I reached for the light.

"Good night, Livvie," my dad called from across the hall.

"Good night."

"Good night," my mom said.

"Good ni-ight," Mark crooned from behind his closed door. "Good night, John-Boy, good night, Mary Ellen."

"Shut uu-up," I sang back.

Then I slid one hand between my thighs, pressing a finger, touching myself through the flannel of my pajamas. It was nice to do this at home, alone in my room, without worrying about making the bunk springs squeak or waking Andrea. I found the spot, slipped my hand under the elastic waistband and into my underwear. I imagined someone else's hand there, lips kissing me while a warm finger slid in and out of my wetness. "Yes. There," I would whisper. Our legs would snake together, urgent and hot.

Once, the first week of school, I was home on a Friday night, eating Entenmann's chocolate chip cookies and touching myself under the afghan, when Andrea stumbled in. I shoved the cookies under the covers. Andrea was flushed, with a tail of mascara hanging from each eye.

"I had sex with some guy—I don't even know his last name,"

she blurted. "We were dancing and then I was in his room, and I thought about saying no, but then it all felt so good, and he was being really sweet, you know, saying things about my hair and stuff, and one thing just led to another. Do you think I'm a terrible person?"

"No," I said honestly. "No, I don't."

She looked at me, then rolled her eyes. "Oh, why the hell am I telling you? You've probably never even finger-fucked."

The light went out in my parents' room, and I could hear the bed creak as they rolled toward each other. My sheets had the vanilla smell I remembered from childhood. I hoped Mark wasn't still awake. I turned over, facedown, with my head on the pillow, and rocked on my hand, back and forth, back and forth, until a wave lifted me weightless and carried me quivering up, up, up and over, over the edge, and dropped me into a dense and dreamless sleep.

I woke up hungry and queasy at the same time. From across the room I could see the Archway cookie package in the trash. I walked over and fished it out. Three left. I put two of them in my mouth at once, like a sandwich, and chewed. One more. What the hell? I could start tomorrow, back at school, diet Coke all day, no more peanut butter and jelly sandwiches, only low-fat dressing at the salad bar. I folded the last cookie in half and ate it quickly, then pleated the cardboard and cellophane into a tiny package and stuffed it in the pocket of my coat.

When I packed up my books, I saw that my dad had left me a note: "Hi, sweetheart, sorry I left too early to see you this morning. Congratulations on the *A* in Shakespeare. Not surprised, though. If you put that same discipline into losing weight, I know you could do it. Love, Dad."

I stuck it between the pages of Aristotle.

Downstairs, my mother was reading the science section and drinking tea. "Want any breakfast?" she asked. "There's cereal, eggs, bagels . . ."

"No, thanks. I'm still full from dinner. . . . Hey, Mom?"

"Yes?"

"What did Nana and Pop do when you couldn't stop tying your shoes?"

"Nothing at first. Then they tried to bribe me—an extra piece of mandelbrot if I'd stop. Then they got worried. And finally, Nana and Tanta Zena took me to someone."

"Like a shrink?"

"No, not a shrink. More like a . . . well, I guess you'd call him an exorcist, although Jews don't really believe in exorcism. Kind of a sorcerer."

"What did he do?"

"Well, he took me into the kitchen—it was one of those tiny little row houses, with the kitchen way in the back—and he picked up an egg and moved it around over my head, and said some things, and announced I was cured."

"And?"

"And I stopped tying my shoes."

"That's it?"

She shrugged. "Whatever it was, I guess it worked."

"Don't you remember anything else? What he said? Was it Hebrew or Yiddish or English? Were you scared?"

"I honestly don't remember, honey. I don't think I was scared."

"Mom, it's important. How can you not remember? I mean,

you were tying your shoes a million times a day, you were this crazy little kid, and then some guy says magic words, and, poof, you're cured, no more obsession?"

"Mmm-hmm. Funny, isn't it? Now, with everything we know about psychology . . ."

"No, it isn't funny. I don't think it's funny," and suddenly I was crying, just standing there in the kitchen with my eyes burning and snot coming out of my nose. It seemed like forever, but it was probably only a few seconds, until my mother got up from her chair, walked over, and embraced me, her two hands straining to meet each other across my back.

Aggiornamento

Claudia Miceli was born in a wash of tears on the afternoon that news of Vatican II spread through South Philadelphia like word of a basil blight. Claudia's father, Guiseppe, whose customers called him Joe, stood at his stall in the Italian Market, third from the corner of Ninth and Catherine, on the shady side of the street, carefully stacking pears so the soft spots faced the back. His transistor radio—which earlier that year had burst with news of Jackie Robinson's election to Baseball's Hall of Fame and the Supreme Court's banning of school prayer—now crackled again with the important, long-distance sound of change.

Pope John XXIII was calling for *aggiornamento*. Modernization of the church in light of the changing times. Involvement of the laity. Mass in the vernacular.

"Hey, Joe," called his cousin Louis Grillo from the next stall. Lou consistently undercut Joe's prices, but he couldn't match his cousin's painterly eye, his vivid rows of broccoli, golden peppers, purple cabbage. "Mass in the vernacular? What the hell part of the church is that?" Before Joe could answer, his left thumb pressed right through the brown stain on the side of a Comice pear. It was pulpy to the core.

On the street's sunny side and three floors up, in a small bedroom filled with calla lilies and opera music because the midwife believed they helped ease the pains of birth, the radio station interrupted its broadcast of Pavarotti to describe the opening sessions of the Ecumenical Council. The midwife was thinking that *aggiornamento* sounded like a kind of sweet dessert cheese, and that she would miss the tidal rhythms of Gregorian chants. Just then, Susanna Miceli groaned, and a dripping, crinkled infant slipped into the midwife's hands.

"Ay, *una figlia*. A daughter." The fathers paid more for delivering a boy. She turned the baby over—hair the color of Calamata olives, limbs folded like a chicken, and eyes streaming with tears. "Claudia," murmured Susanna from the sheets. "Claudia Catherine Miceli." From the paper-thin sound of Susanna's voice and the bluish tint to skin that should have been flushed peach, the midwife knew that Susanna would not live long enough to wean the baby.

"*Non piangere*," she counseled the wailing infant. "Later, plenty time for tears. Don't cry, *mia cara bambina*." As the midwife wrapped her in a blanket, the baby seemed to measure the room with her wet green eyes, taking in the bars of sunlight, the candid mouths of the calla lilies, the calendar of saints. It was October 11, 1962. This is a wise one, the midwife thought. Claudia wept, as if for all that had happened during the nine months she bobbed in the sea sac of Susanna's belly: tears of grief for the two Flying Wallendas who faltered off the high wire in Detroit and died, and tears of hope for the college students whose chants for peace were ringed with white huffs of breath as they marched near the White House in February. Surely, the midwife thought, she was not crying for Salvatore "Lucky" Luciano, the mob boss who keeled over from a heart attack on his way to discuss a movie about his life with a Hollywood producer.

The midwife nodded. A wise one. The world was whispering open; the world was a throat closed tight. Claudia sobbed for the ones who would die before it was clear whether sound or silence would prevail. She cried for her mother, whose sleepy fingers drew patterns on her daughter's still-wet head. If Susanna lived, she would be back in this bed to push another infant into the world in a year or so, and Claudia sensed that her own birth had scraped the bottom of Susanna's scant reservoir of strength. Still, she was pragmatic enough to suck greedily at what milk Susanna had, while soaking eleven brand-new diapers with her tears.

On the radio, in a speech transmitted through miles of salty ocean, the Pope said, "At the present moment in history, Providence is leading us toward a new order in human relations." Downstairs, Joe shrugged in Lou Grillo's direction and wiped his sticky thumb on a piece of newspaper. And across town, in a room no larger than a closet, a young Sister of Mercy took shears to her black serge habit and smiled as she cut a generous seven inches from the hem.

As the midwife and Claudia had anticipated, Susanna did not last long. She seemed to lose a pound for each one the baby gained, and her milk soon dried to a trickle. Nothing worked: not medicinal teas, garlic broths, or the desperate prayers Joe uttered each day, directing them not skyward but east, toward Lou's tumbled display, the Delaware River, and, far beyond that, he guessed and hoped, to Rome, where the assemblage of three thousand clerics must carry as much clout as God.

Claudia was six months old when Susanna died, and Joe held his daughter gently as a bunch of new greens, tucking her into his raincoat at the graveside service. Afterward, his sisters offered to take the child—what's one more mouth at a noisy table?—but Joe refused to give her up. The baby's smell, chamomile and toast, reminded him of Susanna, and when he held the wailing infant close to his face to soothe her, a sweet liquor of tears clung to his chin.

Claudia sat in a stroller behind Joe's stand every day, listening to the radio. She cried in despair when Kitty Genovese was murdered, her New York neighbors shutting their windows to her dying screams. And she giggled, tears of delight plinking musically onto the sidewalk, when the Supremes' single, "Where Did Our Love Go?" soared to the Top 40. But she did not speak, not for two whole years, until the day when twenty-three women auditors, by invitation only, joined the third session of Vatican II.

"Listen, Papa," she said on that afternoon when bishops were cringing across the sea. "Listen radio." Joe turned up the volume. According to the broadcast, several progressive bishops had actually welcomed the women, referring to these silent observers as "*sorores admirandae*"—"admirable sisters"—and "*pulcherrimae auditrices*"—"most beautiful female auditors."

"Ladies at the Vatican, I don't know." Lou shook his head. "Next thing, it'll be nuns in miniskirts. Then again, maybe that wouldn't be so bad, huh, Joe?" But Joe was watching his daughter. She leaned toward the radio the way some people arch forward in prayer, as if she expected to hear the women speaking all the way from Rome. "*Sorores admirandae,*" Claudia repeated, as if it were a lullaby, tears streaking her face. Then she reached out one small puckered hand. "Papa, orange." Joe peeled it as shyly as if he were making love.

As Claudia grew, she spent each day after school with Joe at his market stall, listening to the shouts of the men: "Getcher greens here, nice greens. Cu-CUM-bers, five f'ra dolla. C'mon, darlin', you never had berries so sweet. The whole flat—for you, hon, three bucks." Claudia watched the way Joe piled the soft berries on the bottom and the plumpest ones on top, how he stacked the eggplants bruised side down. The customers were changing: everyone in a rush, the younger women running past at five o'clock with bags of frozen supermarket peas. One day, an entire case of broccoli arrived spoiled, the stems brown and the florets mossy. When Joe tried to trim out the usable parts, Claudia sat on the sour curb and burst into tears.

"Whatsa matter, sweetheart, you don't like to work?" Joe pleaded. "You want I should leave you home? This is my business, was my papa's business before me. I don't have no son to take over. So I want you should watch how I do, how I make do, okay?"

Through a drapery of tears, Claudia watched. She saw the old woman who longed for portobello mushrooms but had money only for leeks and navy beans. She saw the father who held his son's hand so tightly, he ruined the grip; the boy would never be able to hold on to money or love. She grew pale when Gladys Leoni dropped a carton of eggs on the sidewalk, a dozen shivering yellow planets. By twelve, she could make change and gauge

26

the weight of a cabbage in one hand; as she worked, her tears poured over the broad green leaves of chard, spilled in rivers through the radishes, dripped over the mushrooms in their crates, washing off the crumbs of dirt and leaving moist white knobs.

Claudia wept each day as she read the newspaper—when ten thousand women marched down Fifth Avenue shouting "E-R-A! E-R-A!"; when Janis Joplin died of an overdose; when Karen Silkwood's car crashed on her way to tell the reporter what was wrong at the plutonium plant. By the time she finished with the *Bulletin*, it was a pulpy mass, the ink bleeding over her fingers and the words clotted on her blouse like lint.

Joe, whose father had prepared him well for the business of selling produce but not at all for the infinite emotional shades of parenthood, did not know what to think about his daughter's tears. He had begun to notice that the more Claudia cried over the vegetables, the better they looked. Joe's broccoli was brighter, his peas plumper, his eggplants glossier than anyone else's. Her tears rained slugs out of the radicchio and cleaned the carrots so thoroughly that they did not need to be peeled. But even his regular customers grew wary and steered their baskets around the girl with the flooded green eyes, the women uttering a brief "*Santo Dio*" as they eyed Joe's glistening produce with longing and fear.

Except for Rosemary Petrazzi, the pale and agitated wife of Frank Petrazzi, who ran the funeral home. Each day, Rosemary approached Joe's stand, blinked at each vegetable, then purchased a single item, pointing with her eggshell hands—a bunch of celery, a cluster of radishes, a solitary golden pepper. Claudia carefully chose the prettiest one, then bagged the item and handed it across the table.

"Thank you," Rosemary said quietly. "*Mille grazie*. Thank you." Claudia nodded, brine spilling onto her cheeks.

Lou shook his head. "You oughta put a pail under that kid, catch the water case we ever have a drought." It was obvious that Joe's business was failing. The vegetables gleamed so richly, they seemed to be lit from within, but they lay there all day, untouched, purple and green and orange, shining like angels, until Joe rolled up the awning and frowned at his near-empty till. So, late at night, in the corners of certain dim taverns after the bartender's last call, Joe began to confer in low voices with Lou and Ernie Baldinucci and a few others who never seemed to be short of cash. Their talk was of horses, or a pretty widow with something she needed to sell, or, when they hunched their shoulders and dropped their voices the lowest, of someone who, Christ Almighty, needed to be taught a lesson.

Joe confessed these sins selectively each week: "Pardon me, Father, for I have coveted . . . I have lied . . . I have taken the Lord's name in vain." His true business was fruits and vegetables, and he assumed God and the ghost of his sainted father understood the bind he was in. He couldn't fire his own daughter. Nor could he persuade anyone but Rosemary Petrazzi that his produce wasn't possessed.

One Thursday, while Claudia was still in school, Rosemary took even longer than usual to choose a leafy bouquet of broccoli rabe. "Mr. Petrazzi," she began. "My . . . my husband. He needs criers. At the funeral home. He can pay. It's steady work. Maybe your daughter . . ." Then she seemed to run out of breath. Lou was leaning over his scale to hear.

"Should I let her do it?" Joe asked him.

"Why not? She cries like a fountain anyway; this way, it shouldn't go to waste." Joe nodded as he handed Rosemary her change. If Claudia worked for Petrazzi, maybe he could hire his eager nephew, Mark, and get some of the business back. He told Claudia that afternoon, and she wept, though he could not say whether her tears were of terror or relief.

Here's what I need." Mr. Petrazzi smelled of embalming fluid, cheap suits, and domestic cigars. "Some funerals, the person was so fine, so upstanding, the relatives can't stop themselves wailing. But others . . . well, maybe he was a little bit of a cheat, or maybe she was not so nice to her sisters, there's not a damp hankie in the place. It doesn't look good. So we hire you to sit in the back and cry up a storm. Make the dead guy think somebody's gonna miss him. Make the relatives feel better, their dearly departed wasn't such a louse after all. Sometimes you get a little tear out of one or two distant cousins. It's contagious, see, like a yawn."

"Okay," said Claudia.

"Okay? That's all? Okay, then. Ten dollars a funeral, twelve if it's a Mass, takes up more of your time. Five for a wake. You can start tomorrow, two o'clock. A Mr. Ed Torani. Landlord. Ah, slumlord, really. Tenants hated him. Wife not too fond of him, either. No kids. We'll need you."

And so Claudia left her father's failing produce stall at the age of fifteen and became a hired crier. Wearing a black crepe dress that had been her mother's, her chin modestly tucked and a handkerchief concealed in one sleeve, she slipped in after the mourners and sat in the third pew from the back. Light from the clerestory windows oozed across her lap like melting cheese. She thought about those college students killed in Ohio, their shocked bodies on the front of the newspaper. She thought about the buckets of crabs, still half-alive, that arrived at the market each morning, their claws scraping the tin buckets in a panic.

Then she felt the bubble swell at the base of her throat, a hot throb behind her eyes, the wet itch in her nose that couldn't be scratched, could only be flushed away. A tourniquet drew taut around her head, and her chest squeezed shut as she opened her mouth to that first pull of air that came in dry and went out wet. One tear stung a path down the side of her nostril, to rest hotly on her lip. The next tears came more easily and seemed less saline, like the water that runs pumpkin-colored from a rusty faucet and gradually clears. Her throat opened in sobs that sounded like the ripping of taffeta, her whole body a damp pocket turned inside out. Mr. Petrazzi nodded happily in her direction.

After the service, Claudia sat for a minute, her body still shaky with tears. Rosemary Petrazzi appeared at the end of the pew. "Come. I have soup." She curled a finger, a parenthesis riding the air. Claudia followed her up a flight of dark stairs above the funeral parlor, where a door opened to the apartment's rear entrance, a kitchen humid with roasting garlic, thick with the burgundy perfume of minestrone. They sat at a Formica table, spooning soup from heavy white bowls, smiling at each other through the blur of steam.

In her own kitchen, Rosemary was calm as a shadow. She taught Claudia how to use the big chef's knife, so sharp that slicing an onion was like spooning through a dish of gelato, so fast that the onion was sizzling in the pot before its stinging cologne could reach her eyes. They made black bean soup, pureed by hand until it turned the grainy purple-brown of melted chocolate, and rosemary focaccia that ballooned out of the bowl before they plunged their fists in, giggling as the dough sighed flat. Claudia began to linger after each Mass, searching the shadowed rear pews for Rosemary's pale face, her quick, expectant motion toward the stairs.

"Where did you learn to cook?" Claudia asked one day.

"In the convent."

"You were a nun?" The only nuns Claudia knew were the serene gray-suited teachers at St. Cecilia's. Her cousins had told her terrible stories about the old nuns, the ones whose stern portraits lined the corridors, stories of endless Latin drills and rulers that left hot crimson welts. The sisters used to wear cornets, the fluted hats that made kids call them "God's geese" behind their monumental backs.

"I wanted to be," Rosemary said. "It was so quiet in the convent. Prayers and singing. Scrub the floor on my knees until it looked like glass. Peel two hundred potatoes for the sisters' lunch. I knew how to do things. God's work. I was so happy to be there."

"Why didn't you stay?"

Just then, the main door of the apartment sprang open, and the mellow odors of garlic and rising bread were cut by something chemical and sharp. Rosemary flinched, then drew her hand to her mouth. The big knife clattered to the floor.

"Did I surprise you? Sorry." Mr. Petrazzi picked up the knife, smiled at Claudia, and reached for his wife's hand. There was a

31

scribble of blood on her thumb. "Here, let me see." But Rosemary shook her head. "You're doing a fine job," he said to Claudia. "No, I mean that. Best little crier I've ever had. How come you got so much tears inside, huh? Guess it's none of my business, right? You ladies have your secrets."

"You should go," Rosemary said to Claudia, and nodded toward the back stairs. From below, in the room where Mr. Petrazzi raised the lids of caskets to show stunned families their expensive satin linings, Claudia could hear heavy steps in the kitchen, a thick voice saying, "Please, let me see. Come on, *cara mia*, let me kiss it, make it better."

"No, it's fine. I'm fine. Don't. No—let go. Please! Let go!" Rosemary said, and then Claudia heard her quick steps on the kitchen floor, vanishing toward the far end of the apartment.

Joe's customers began to return, though a few of the women crossed themselves before picking up a cucumber or a bunch of escarole. The vegetables looked normal again, and Joe taught his nephew how to conceal the brown-fringed basil sprigs in the center of the bunch, how to insist a cantaloupe would ripen in time for Sunday dinner.

Meanwhile, Claudia became an expert. She wept at the passing of mob hit men and petty thieves, of women who'd never hugged their children and men who had not once said a kind word to their mothers. She cried through the burials of cops and aldermen, seamstresses and butchers, nurses, janitors, and deacons. She wept at the wake of a gambler so lacking in scruples that his own brothers refused to serve as pallbearers. She grieved at the service of a teacher who had once ripped a student's drawing to shreds. She grew so good at it that she had only to glimpse a black hat with a chapel veil or hear the opening notes of "Ave Maria" in order to feel the wet, urgent pulse behind her eyes.

But as the months passed, she rarely shed an honest tear. As she ran up the street, late for the wake of a City Council member who had been siphoning money out of construction contracts for years to finance visits to a certain house of ill repute, Claudia half-heard a radio report about the Jim Jones followers who had drunk cyanide-laced Kool-Aid in Guyana. Her eyes stayed dry. Nor did she cry the following March when the nuclear power plant leaked and all the pregnant women had to leave their homes. The world sighed open; the world clammed shut. At work, Claudia wept so efficiently that Mr. Petrazzi offered her a raise.

"Come here," he said one day after a viewing. "I want you should see something." He pulled a glossy box from under his desk, opened it, and held up a satin peignoir. He grasped it by the narrow shoulder straps, holding it far away from his body, as if it were wet and might drip on him.

"Now, you're a pretty girl; you know what pretty girls like. I got this for Rosemary—for Mrs. Petrazzi. She doesn't go in too much for fancy stuff, but I thought this was real nice. You think she'll like it? Tell me the truth."

The peignoir was cloud-colored, a skin of silk. Claudia wanted to touch it, wanted to feel it on her face like rain. A sluice of memory: a tickle of fingers across her forehead; a reverent, weary hand tracing the outline of a tiny ear, guiding her mouth to a sweet, full breast. Claudia's throat filled with feathers. Her eyes were stone. She knew Rosemary would never wear it, and the shiny box would draw a cloak of dust on the top shelf of the hall closet.

"It's nice," she told Mr. Petrazzi, and ran from the room.

Outside the door, she could hear Rosemary come down from the apartment.

"Look what I got you," Mr. Petrazzi said. "For Valentine's Day. Hold it up; let me see how it looks. . . . Come on. Rosemary, just hold it."

"No," Rosemary was saying, her voice barely a rustle. "No, I promised. You know I can't. . . ."

"I'm so sick of your goddamn promise. You promised me, too. In the church, remember? You said, 'I do.' In front of the Father and God and everyone. Remember, Rosemary? Do you?"

"*Elegi abiecta esse in domo Domini*," Rosemary murmured. "I have chosen to be abject in the house of the Lord."

"Shut up," Mr. Petrazzi yelled.

"*Elegi abiecta esse —*"

"Shutupshutupshutup!" He hiccuped wetly. Claudia bent down and looked through the keyhole. Mr. Petrazzi pressed his hands to his eyes, and the silver peignoir shuddered to the floor.

In a test tube in a British laboratory, cells danced minuets, and the first baby conceived outside the womb was born. Claudia did not weep with awe or trepidation. The next winter, three American nuns were killed in El Salvador. Briefly, she pictured their cornets flattened in the street like run-over pigeons. Then she took her usual spot, this time at the funeral of a man who had kept his dog chained to the kitchen table, her shoulders spasmic with grief, while the family glared dry-eyed over their hymnals.

Upstairs, she watched Rosemary slice carrots into even, lengthwise strips, the heavy knife blade thwacking the board. In spite of the sticky August afternoons, Rosemary had begun to wear her habit—the dress, not the veil—from her convent days, its dark hem brushing the kitchen floor, the long sleeves grazing her wrists. She repeated the story Claudia had heard many times.

"I wanted to stay in the convent forever. My father made me leave. To get married. Mr. Petrazzi was a friend of his." She turned the carrot slices and clipped them into tidy matchsticks. "He made me leave, but he couldn't make me break my vows. You know Father Gano? He lets me clean the church. After the Mass. I wear white gloves to polish the chalice. But I don't touch the altar cloths, not until Father rinses them. Because I might be unclean. I polish everything until it shines. Like your father's vegetables." She turned to Claudia. "That's how I knew. That you were one. *Carissima sorore.* Dearest sister. Did God call you, too?"

Heavy steps began to clomp up the main stairs, and Rosemary pushed Claudia to the door. "Another time," she whispered, tugging her long sleeves down over the blue-black smudges on her hands. Then she turned, using her knife to part the face of a cabbage into a perfect grid.

It was early, too early, even, for the most aggressive sellers to be haggling down at the produce warehouse, when Joe nudged Claudia from sleep. "I got a call, sweetheart. Very sudden. They need you. The funeral home. It's . . . Petrazzi." Claudia pulled on her black dress and ran. Mr. Petrazzi wasn't so old—did he have a heart attack? A stroke? Or maybe Rosemary did it; maybe they'd fought and she'd hurt him, accidentally, with the knife. Maybe something went bad in the soup; maybe she knew and served it anyway, and he'd died at the table, both hands grasping his throat.

But it was Mr. Petrazzi who met her at the door as usual, his face slack and sweating. "Oh God," he said. "She fell. She was always so clumsy, dropping and falling and . . . well, there ain't much family. Just you, really . . ." and he motioned Claudia into the casket room.

Rosemary lay in an oak box. The room smelled strange, a tulle of gardenias over a stink of smoke. A young priest was murmuring prayers in the corner. Claudia leaned over the coffin, trying to coax tears from the husks of her lungs, willing them to drop like pearls from the corners of her eyes. Nothing. Tomorrow the coffin would lie at the altar, lit with candles whose holders Rosemary had polished with her bruised, gloved hands.

Kitty Genovese and Karen Silkwood and Rosemary Petrazzi and Susanna were dead, but it wasn't over yet. Women had been wailing for centuries, millennia; this time, Claudia thought, someone would listen. There was a chatter of static overhead, like the radio before a broadcast, and a restless undulation at Claudia's feet, and the room seemed to lean ever so slightly forward.

Then a sound broke loose from the bottom of her throat, a sound like a button sprung from its anchor thread, a shirt shucked off on the first warm day of spring. Her ribs spread wide, and she giggled to relieve the pressure rising in her chest. The priest lost his place and glanced up with a frown. Claudia's giggles widened into a full laugh, spilling through the fingers she had clapped to her mouth, a percussive, bubbling laugh that went on for minutes. The priest stumbled in his prayer: "Our Mother, who art in heaven," he murmured, then grew pale and fled the room.

Claudia's laughter churned and tumbled, blew from the windows like colored flags, flounced over the cobblestones, rolled toward the river. It curdled the alfredo sauce in Baldinucci's restaurant kitchen and turned his onions black in their papery coats. It fizzed through the doors of the public library, where a girl approaching confirmation read all she could find and decided she would definitely take Philip as her saint's name.

A flock of geese arched their wings and rose from the pond in back of St. Cecilia's Academy, where two senior girls lay in a brandy puddle of sunlight, their fingers entwined, laughing about how much the birds resembled the nuns' old hats. Downtown, a certain Mary O'Connor tucked a diaphragm into her wedding-night suitcase. And up and down the stalls at the market, Joe and Lou and the other men jumped back, their hands stained red and dripping as, one by one, the tomatoes burst their skins.

The Whole Truth and Nothing But

The McReddys had rules.

No bare feet at breakfast. No singing at the table. Everyone got a glass of orange juice in a sweating green tumbler, and we kids got glasses of milk, too. You had to eat all your Cream of Wheat before you could have a Pop-Tart. And if you pushed the Cream of Wheat around with your spoon, making it into the Andes Mountains you'd just learned about in Ms. Genova's eighth-grade social studies class, you got a sour look from Mrs. McReddy.

I lifted a small spoonful of the white goop to my mouth and swallowed, washing it down with a gulp of juice. "I'm glad to see that Vaneesa appreciates her breakfast," Mrs. McReddy said, nodding at me. "But it looks to me like someone else is playing with her food."

Then, if you pushed it some more and said, "Looks to me like throw-up," really quietly under your breath, your mother called you by your full name, Cornelia Bernardine McReddy, in a voice like scissors, and you got sent straight to your room.

That happened the first time I stayed over at Corrie and Jenny's, a couple weeks into eighth grade. Even though I was a year younger, I was in Corrie's class because I'd skipped kindergarten. At first, the school thought it was a bad idea, since I wasn't even five yet, but my parents insisted, then proved their point by dragging me into the principal's office and making me read out loud from *Wuthering Heights*.

Ever since, I'd gotten *A*'s without really trying, but with the other kids, I felt like I was an hour late for the movie. I still loved my argyle kneesocks when the other girls started buying panty hose in plastic eggs; I knew all the lyrics to Partridge Family songs when they began listening to Jethro Tull. Sometimes Corrie gave me advice, like to watch Marcus Welby and quit using those plastic barrettes. Sometimes she ignored me. This was one of the good weeks. She'd even promised to show me how to put on eye shadow.

After Corrie ran upstairs, her slippers going *thwip, thwip* on each wooden step, her mother handed a plate of sausage links around the table.

"I'll pass on the dead animal meat," Jenny said. She was ten, two years younger than me, dark-haired and sooty-eyed, not like the rest of the freckled, pale McReddys. My mother said she was precocious.

"Just say 'No thank you,' " her mother said. "Anyway, you don't know what you're missing." Jenny started clanging her spoon against her juice glass and singing. "Great green gobs of greasy grimy gopher guts."

"That's enough, Jennifer," Mr. McReddy said.

"Mutilated monkey meat," Jenny sang softly.

"I said, that will be enough, Jennifer Ann."

"Stinky slimy spider feet." It was almost a whisper.

"Jennifer Ann McReddy, cut that out!" And he reached across the table to grab her wrist. Jen flicked his hand away, knocking over both her juice glass and her milk glass at the same time. They sploshed over the table, across my plate, and into my lap, rivers of orange and white like a melted Creamsicle. Jenny was like that: the kind of kid who made things happen. I was the kind they happened to.

"Go to your room this instant," said Mrs. McReddy, and jumped up to get a sponge.

That left me sitting there, my robe cold and sticking to my pajamas, my Cream of Wheat hardening like papier-mâché in the bowl, the McReddys pink-faced and silent.

It was different at my house.

"Do you ever get in trouble?" Corrie asked the first time she slept over. We'd played parachute jumpers, squeezing ourselves between the bars of the banister, holding pillowcases over our heads and bouncing down to the couch below. We'd slid down the stairs in sleeping bags and dressed each other in my mom's old clothes and makeup.

"My mom'd kill me if I used her rouge," Corrie said, smearing big circles of it on both cheeks. "Can we go up in the attic?"

"Sure," I said.

"Don't you have any rules?"

I thought for a minute. I went to bed when I got tired. I didn't have to finish all my food and, sometimes, if my parents were having leg of lamb or scallops, I ate cinnamon toast for dinner. My parents' rules—"Don't say hate"; "Always look for the good in people"; and "Tell us when you're upset about something"— didn't seem like real rules, more like some kind of religion. If I forgot to hug my grandmother good-bye or called my little brother "fart breath," no one said my whole name or sent me to my room. Instead, my mother or father would get a sad look and say, "Neesa, I'm disappointed in you."

Finally, I thought of one. "Don't put shoes on the bed." It wasn't really a rule, more like a superstition, but my mom would throw a fit and grab my sneakers off the comforter if I forgot.

Corrie looked at me, her face a perfect peach with two brown stones for eyes. "That is so dumb. Who would put shoes on the bed, anyway? Hey, let's go make experiments with the stuff in the bathroom."

"Okay," I said.

That morning at the McReddys', I wondered what room they would send me to if I misbehaved.

"What time are your parents getting home, dear?" Mrs. McReddy asked. I didn't know. Then no one said anything. I could hear the refrigerator purring, the cat crunching Friskies in the corner. When Mrs. McReddy turned to squeeze out the sponge and Mr. McReddy unfolded the newspaper as if he'd been waiting to do that all along, I grabbed a Pop-Tart from the plate in the middle and slipped it into the pocket of my robe.

"May I please be excused?" I asked.

"Yes, dear, you may," said Mrs. McReddy. She sounded relieved.

I took the stairs two at a time and stood in front of Corrie and Jenny's door. The upper panel, which belonged to Corrie, was covered with pictures of Donny Osmond and sheets of notebook paper that said "Enter at Your Own Risk" in orange crayon. The lower half, Jenny's part of the door, had a picture of Joan Baez, a poem by Kahlil Gibran, and a small poster that said WAR IS NOT HEALTHY FOR CHILDREN AND OTHER LIVING THINGS.

I knocked on Corrie's half. "Go away," she said. Her voice sounded wet and hiccupy.

"Corrie, I snuck you a Pop-Tart. Want it?"

"Why don't you just go downstairs and suck up to my parents some more? Maybe they'll adopt you."

"Corrie, come on, let me in." I heard a sniffle. "Want me to slide it under?"

"I don't care," Corrie said.

I took the Pop-Tart out of my robe and crouched down to poke it under the door. "Sorry it's a little wet. Jenny's juice and milk spilled on it."

"Jenny is a stupid spaz," Corrie said, and then two long fingers, olive-skinned and with no nail polish, so I knew they couldn't be Corrie's, wiggled through and pulled the Pop-Tart to the other side.

"Thanks," Jen said. "I was starving."

I sat down in the hall and stared at the orange stain on my robe.

There was another rule at the McReddys'. Never let anyone see you cry.

A few months later, I crashed Corrie's thirteenth-birthday sleep-over. She was in one of her hating-me phases, ever since I'd used the word *appropriate* in an oral book report. "Ap-pro-pri-ate," she'd sneer at my back. "My, isn't that dress ap-pro-pri-ate?"

It was actually my mom who made me crash the party. She and my dad decided to be spontaneous and fly to San Francisco for their fifteenth anniversary, so she asked the McReddys if I could stay the night. Mrs. McReddy said that was fine and, what

a coincidence, it just happened to be Corrie's birthday and she
was having a little party. My mom packed my stuff—a pair of
those footed pajamas my grandma was always sending, my tooth-
brush, a towel—into a pink plaid suitcase, but I took it all out and
put it into a grocery bag instead.

"I don't have a present to give her," I complained. "Can't I just
stay here and get a baby-sitter? Corrie doesn't want me at her
party. If she did, she would have invited me in the first place."

"Of course she wants you there. Mrs. McReddy said so." My
mom rummaged around in her studio and found a new pad of
drawing paper and a set of thirty-two pastels. "Here, we can wrap
these up."

"Corrie hates to draw." I knew the others would give her stuff
like friendship rings and lip gloss and necklaces with her name
spelled out in lacy script. I stuck the present in the bag, on top of
my clothes.

Mr. McReddy opened the front door and pointed me up to
Corrie and Jenny's room.

"Friendofo?" someone said when I knocked, and then there
was a spurt of giggling.

"What?"

"Friend or foe?" the voice repeated.

"Um, friend, I guess."

"That's for us to decide," Corrie said, and the door swung
open. The room smelled of cherry bubble gum and something
else I couldn't figure out. Jenny sat curled on her bed in the corner, reading. The others—Corrie, Michelle DiLillo, and Suzan
Carr—were sitting on the rug. Michelle wasn't in our class, but I
knew her from church; she always got picked to be St. Lucia and

carry the wreath of candles through the dark aisle. Suzan had thick brown hair cut in a wedge and wore pink hoop earrings the size of bracelets. Kids at school said she was fast.

The three of them had been friends ever since first grade. Sometimes they made plans to wear the exact same clothes—say, a green plaid skirt with navy tights and penny loafers—and then squealed when they spotted one another in the hall, like it had all been one big accident.

"We're playing Truth or Dare," Michelle said. She wore a flannel nightgown with a design of tiny blue hearts on it; Corrie and Suzan had on oversized T-shirts and underpants.

I put my paper bag down on the green shag carpet. "I have something for you," I said, and handed Corrie the packages.

"Well, I know it's not records," she said, and tore off the wrapping. "Oh, drawing paper. And crayons. So I can color in the lines, right?"

"They're pastels."

"Cool," Jen said from her corner.

"Who asked you? Anyway, they're mine. I'll kill you if you touch them. Thanks, Neesa," she said, and slid the boxes under her dresser. "So, are you playing Truth or Dare with us or not?"

"Is Jenny playing?"

"Jenny is a pissant. She just wants to read her important book," Corrie said. "Right, Jen, darling sister of mine?"

Jenny narrowed her eyes to dark slots. "I didn't even want to come to your stupid party, but Mom said I had to. And you better leave me alone, or I'll tell Dad you took a bottle out of his liquor cabinet."

"You do, and I'll break your neck."

"Ooh, I'm so scared," Jenny said, but she moved closer to the wall and burrowed between two pillows.

Then Corrie was back to business. "Neesa, it's your turn. Truth or dare?"

I thought a minute. Truth seemed risky. I never seemed to know the right answers to Corrie's questions, like that time two years ago when she asked if I was a virgin, and I thought she meant Virgo, like the horoscope. My birthday's in November. "No," I said, "but my mom is." Corrie laughed so hard, she almost choked, and I still felt my insides go hot and waxy when I thought about it.

They were waiting. At least a dare would be over fast, and I might not have to talk.

"Dare," I said.

"Let's start with an easy one," Suzan said. "Change into your pajamas right here in front of us, with the lights on." Corrie leaned over and whispered something in Suzan's ear that made her laugh. Michelle blew a huge pink bubble and popped it with a finger. Then they all stared at me like I was the television set.

Suzan started humming a striptease song: "Da-da-DAH-da-da-da-DAH . . ." while I tugged my sweater over my head. It got caught on my glasses, and I had to reach in from the top to pull them out. Then I leaned down, nudged my sneakers off, and peeled down both blue kneesocks. My shins were white as cheese.

My pajamas were the zip-up kind, with vinyl soles on the feet, like babies wear. I had a whole cabinet full of them, in different colors and patterns. "Oh, great, look what my mom packed," I said, pulling the pajamas out of the bag and holding them away from me as if they smelled. Actually, these were my favorites, with black-and-white diamonds like the harlequin in a play my parents took me to see.

"Your *mom* packed your stuff?" Suzan said.

"Well, just tonight, because I was in a rush. Anyway—" and I quickly unbuttoned my jeans, pushed them down, and stepped out of them. I reached for the pajamas.

"No, you have to take everything off except underpants and stand there while we count to five," Corrie said.

"Wait, that wasn't part of it. You just said change with the lights on, and that's what I'm doing."

"Well, do it, then."

"Okay. Okay." I unbuttoned my blouse and let it fall off my shoulders.

"One," Suzan began, and the others chorused with her, "two, three . . ."

"Look, she hardly has any tits," Corrie said.

"Yeah, but she's got a pretty nice bod. No flab," Suzan said. Michelle just giggled.

"Four," I said.

"*We* do the counting," said Corrie. "Four and a half, four and three-quarters . . ." My toes dug into the thick wool of the carpet. I moved my eyes over the bookcase, the nightstand, anywhere but at the three of them, three sets of headlights bearing down on me. The corner. Jenny sat there with her book lowered, her eyes wide open, not mean and accelerating the way her sister's were, but curious and hopeful, the way you'd read a map to someplace you really want to go.

"Five," they finally chorused, and I slid into my pajamas and zipped them up to my chin.

"Congratulations," Corrie said, and scooted over to make room for me between herself and Michelle. "Who's next?"

"How about the birthday girl?" Suzan said.

Corrie held her hair up in a bunch on top of her head, then let it fall over her face. "Dare."

Michelle and Suzan leaned toward each other and said something in low voices. "Oh, that's good. That's great," Michelle said. "We dare you to go take five dollars out of your mom's purse."

"Cinch," Corrie said. Walking with exaggerated sneaking steps, she opened the door to the burble of the TV downstairs, then closed it behind her. A minute later, she was back, a crumpled five-dollar bill in her hand.

"Ha! Got it."

"Big deal. Once I swiped a fifty from my dad's wallet," said Suzan.

"Sometimes at church, we take money from the collection plate," Michelle said. "Swear you won't tell."

"Never would have guessed it, Saint Michelle," Suzan said. "You're next. Truth or dare?" Michelle twisted the lace on the wrist of her nightgown.

"Dare?" she said, more like a question than an answer.

Suzan stood up and put both hands on Michelle's shoulders, then leaned down to her ear. "Say 'Goddamn fucking Jesus Christ.' "

Michelle turned red. "I can't. That's taking the Lord's name in vain. Think of something else. Come on, Suze." Suzan crossed her arms in front of her chest.

"Nope. That's your dare. Right, girls?"

"Right," Corrie said. My mouth felt papery. Sometimes I said swearwords in the bathroom, with the water running, just to see what they sounded like. "Shit shit shit" while I rinsed my tooth-brush. "Bastard, son of a bitch" while I waited for the tub to fill. But the *F* word scared me, with its hard, grunting edges. When I heard older boys say it, they sounded like they were crunching tiny rocks with their teeth.

I looked at Corrie and Suzan, then at Michelle, who was try-ing to disappear into her nightgown. "Right," I said.

Michelle crossed herself, squeezed her eyes shut, and whis-pered, "Goddamn fucking Jesus Christ."

"Louder," Corrie said. "I couldn't hear you."

Michelle covered her face with both hands. "Goddamn fuck-ing Jesus Christ, goddamn fucking Jesus Christ, GODDAMN FUCKING JESUS CHRIST!" When she took her hands away, her face was splotched white and red, and tears were leaking from both eyes. She wiped them away with her flannel sleeve. No one said anything. I waited to see what would happen next. Corrie picked at the polish on her toenails. Finally, Suzan reached behind her and handed Michelle a pink tissue.

"Here. Don't blow your nose in your nightgown. It's gross. You can ask the next question, if you want."

Michelle sniffled. "I have to think."

Suzan rolled her eyes. "Great, we'll be here all night."

"We *are* going to be here all night," Corrie said, and the two of them started cackling, rolling back and forth on the carpet with their legs waving in the air. Even Michelle started to smile. Then Corrie sat up and said, "Suze, I have one for you while Michelle's thinking. Truth or dare?"

"You know I always take a dare."

"Ohh-kay," Corrie drew out the word like she was pulling

gum from her mouth, sticky and elastic. "Show us all how to put in a Tampax."

"Ewww," Michelle said. "My mom told me a girl shouldn't use those till she's married."

"And you believed her?" Corrie said. "God, you're dumber than I thought. Well, Suzan?"

"No prob, except I didn't exactly pack Tampax in my overnight bag. I'm not on the rag for another week."

"There's some in my mom's—in the bathroom," Corrie said. "Under the sink. Regular and super, scented or not, take your pick."

Suzan hopped up, opened the door, and looked both ways, like she was about to cross the street. Maybe she'd put the Tampax in while she was in the bathroom, then come back and tell us about it. I kind of hoped so. But then she danced into the room, holding up a Tampax, Statue of Liberty–style.

"Ta-dah! Now watch carefully, girls. You might need to do this yourselves someday."

Corrie snorted. "I've had my period three times, Suze. You know that. How about you, Michelle?"

"Just once, three months ago. My mom said that's normal when you're starting."

"Neesa?"

I could lie and say yes, but then they might make me demonstrate, too. I didn't want to remind them I was a year younger. I hated the truth. "Not yet. My mom didn't start till she was fourteen, so I'll probably be late, too. That kind of thing runs in families, you know."

My mother didn't mind talking about stuff like periods. She

told me she didn't like Tampax because they made her feel sort of dried-out inside, but that it would be my choice to use them or not. I'd tried on pads and read the flowered booklet, *Growing Up and Liking It*, about ninety-seven times. Still, I was a little unclear about the details down there, like how I'd know which hole to put the Tampax in, and whether it would hurt, and what if I couldn't find the string again to get it out? The booklet didn't say anything about that.

"Okay, girls, are you taking notes?" Suzan pulled the Tampax out of its paper wrapper. "This end up," she announced like a teacher giving a lecture, "with the string carefully held, like so . . ."

"Oh, gross, I can't look," Michelle said, and ducked her head into the placket of her nightgown.

"It's not gross; it's nat-ur-al," Corrie said. "Come on, Suze, quit playing with it and just put it in."

I glanced up at the corner. Jen was watching us over the edge of her book, but as soon as she saw me looking, she put her eyes down again and turned a page.

Suzan skittered out of her black underpants. Then she squatted a little, and the hand with the Tampax disappeared under the hem of her T-shirt. "So you put one finger on this end and press." She squinted her eyes—"Ow, there it goes"—then opened them and smiled. "And voilà, it's in." She tossed the cardboard tube in the general direction of the wastebasket.

I wished I hadn't seen anything; I wished I'd seen exactly how she did it. I felt the way I did when I cupped my hands over my eyes during *The Exorcist*—can I peek? Can I peek?—and then peeked just as a spurt of green stuff was coming out of the main character's mouth, and felt sick and sorry that I had.

"Can I look now?" Michelle said from inside her nightgown.

"Yeah, yeah. Devirginized before your very eyes. Just kidding, Saint Michelle. So, did you think of one for Neesa yet?"

"I'm not sure if this is really a good one, but—okay, here goes. Neesa, truth or dare?"

This time, I took truth.

"What's the grossest thing you've ever done?"

"Nice one, Michelle." Suzan snapped her fingers, and Corrie snapped hers, too.

The grossest thing? I knew a kid at school, Brad Lafferty, who once swallowed a live tadpole. Michael Morris stabbed his hand with a plastic fork until it bled. I saw Emily Gant take an old piece of gum from under a movie seat and put it in her mouth. But I'd never done anything like that.

I stalled for time. "Gross like . . . a *Friday the Thirteenth* movie, or gross like Mr. Olstein's breath?" Mr. Olstein was our science teacher; he reeked of formaldehyde.

"Gross as in gross," Suzan said. "I'm sure you can think of something *appropriate.*"

Then I remembered the fish. Last spring in North Carolina, I'd gone fishing for the first time—not even real fishing, from a boat, just casting a line off the wet dock behind our rented condominium. My mom helped me hook the worm, but then the phone rang and she went inside to get it.

I felt a pull on my line, and I reeled in, my pole bending toward the water. When the fish lifted from the surface, it just dangled, really quiet and still, and I wondered if it might be dead already. It was silver and blue, a little longer than my hand. I could see the hook poking through one side of its mouth.

I tried to remember any fishing movies I'd seen, but all I could think of were huge heaps of fish, their eyes bugging out, piled on the deck while some guy in yellow boots gave orders. They never showed the unhooking part.

I grabbed the fish in my right hand, and it started twitching and flopping around, the gills gasping open and closed. "I'm sorry, I'm really, really sorry," I said to it. Then I took the hook in my left hand, shut my eyes, and pulled. There was a little ripping noise. I opened my eyes. The hook was in my hand, with a tiny piece of wet fish mouth hanging on it, and the fish was on the deck next to my feet, slapping its tail on the wood. I was too scared to pick it up again, so I just watched it flinch and shudder until my mom came out and threw it back in the bay.

"Come on, we're waiting," Corrie said. "What's the grossest thing you've ever done?"

"I caught a fish."

"Yeah—and?"

"That's it. I took it off the hook. That was kind of gross."

"Ewww," Michelle said. "I could never do that."

Suzan whispered something to Corrie. "Yep, I agree," Corrie said. "We say that answer doesn't qualify. We say you have to do a dare, too. You have to take a swig from the bottle." She reached under her bed and pulled out a tall bottle of brown liquid with a label that said Wild Turkey. I'd had wine before, at dinner with my parents, and I liked the sweet violet taste. One swallow. I could do that.

"If I drink it, it's my last dare," I said.

"Deal," said Corrie.

"Deal." Suzan reached over and shook my hand, hard.

I twisted off the cap and tipped the bottle to my face. My

mouth filled with a musky burning, and some of the liquor dripped onto my pajamas. It tasted worse than any cough medicine, hot red spears plunging into my chest. I licked the last stinging drops off my lips.

"There. I did it. That wasn't so bad, actually."

"Nice job," Suzan said. "Now I've got one more for the birthday girl. Ready, Corrie?"

"Ready and waiting."

"Truth—or dare?"

Corrie leaned forward so her hair fell like a screen in front of her face. "Truth," she said from behind the strands; then she tossed her head back so the hair parted again and settled in a yellow bunch at her shoulders.

"The question is—and you have to tell the truth, remember—have you ever seen your parents do it?"

"Do what?" Michelle asked.

"Oh God, you are so dumb. It, the dirty deed, the nasty, pole in the hole, slam bam thank you ma'am. You know. *Sex.*"

"Oh," said Michelle, and blushed.

"So—have you?" Suzan asked. She was lying on the carpet, with her head propped on a pillow. Corrie hunched her knees up under her T-shirt and stretched the fabric down to cover them. She closed her eyes.

"I haven't seen them, but I've heard them through my wall." She reached out and knocked on the plaster.

"So, what'd you hear?"

"I don't really think we should be talking about this," Michelle said.

"Well, I do. Let's take a vote. Who wants to hear about Corrie's parents doing it?" Suzan raised her own hand. "Corrie obviously wants to tell us. Michelle thinks we should talk about something else, like the Virgin Mary or bunny rabbits. Neesa?"

It was the horror movie all over again. Once you're there, in the movie seat that smells of old popcorn, you can't make the film go backward, or fast-forward through the awful parts. And it's hard to close your eyes to what everyone else is seeing. "I guess," I said, but couldn't look at any of them.

"Sorry, Michelle, you're outvoted. Corrie, tell us the whole thing, what you heard, beginning to end."

"Well, first just kissing sounds. *Smrchh, smrchh.*" Corrie demonstrated on her hand. "Then lots of oohs and moans, and the bed sort of squeaking. Then the oohs and ahs got faster and faster, and my mom was going, 'Oh God, oh Jesus'—sorry, Michelle—and my dad was saying, 'I'm coming, oh, baby, I'm coming,' and then they both sort of screamed at the same time, and that was it."

"Wow," Suzan said. "At the same time?"

I tried to imagine the McReddys in bed together, but I kept seeing them at breakfast, Mr. McReddy behind his wall of newspaper, Mrs. McReddy spooning blobs of Cream of Wheat into bowls. I'd never even seen them kiss. My parents, on the other hand, were always getting mushy. "Smooching," they called it, when I found them cuddling on the living room couch. I asked them to please not do that when my friends were over, but they just laughed. What did they do when I wasn't around, like tonight? Were they making the bed squeak in the hotel in San Francisco?

Michelle scooted over to me and whispered, "What did he mean, 'I'm coming'? Coming where?"

I shrugged.

"No secrets, girls. Care to share with the rest of us?" Michelle looked at her feet. "Neesa? Better answer, or we'll make you do another dare."

"Well, Michelle and I were wondering what that coming part was all about."

"Oh God." Suzan laughed. "Don't you know anything?" She started twisting her butt, grinding her hips and legs against the carpet. "It's like this," she said. " 'Ah, aahhh, aaaaahhhh . . . oh, honey, here I come, I'm coming, I can't stop, oohh, I'm coming.' " Then she flopped her head on the pillow, arms out straight, breathing with her mouth wide open. " Then it's like—'Oh, baby, gimme a cigarette.' "

Corrie was howling by then, rolling back and forth, with her hair flying around like yellow flags. "Yeah, that's how it sounded exactly. 'Oh, ooh, oohhhh God, oh Jesus, oh Holy Mother of Mary, do it to me . . . ' "

Suddenly, there was a snap from the corner, and a dark object sailed through the air, just missing Corrie's head. Jen's book hit the door and fell, its pages flung open. Jen stood on the bed, her eyes like darts. "Liar," she hissed at Corrie. "You are such a liar." Then she jumped down and ran out of the room, grabbing her book on the way. Corrie started to go after her, but Suzan caught the tail of her T-shirt and tugged her back.

"Come on, settle down. Hey, you two, I think it's time to toast Corrie. It's her birthday, right?" She checked her watch. "At least for seven more minutes. Here." And she held up the Wild Turkey.

"To our friend Corrie, may she pass Mrs. Marsh's math class, go to at least second base with Brad Lafferty, and have a great year." She tilted the bottle and took a swig, then handed it to Michelle.

"I don't want any."

"Come on, you've got to. It's a birthday toast." Michelle squeezed her mouth and eyes and lifted the bottle as if it was prune juice. She touched it to her lips, made a face, then said, "Okay, I tasted it." She gave it to me.

"I've had enough." I said, but Suzan pushed the bottle back into my hand. "Do you want Corrie to think you don't like her?" My throat had stopped burning, and a funny feeling had settled in around my head, like when you turn in circles until you fall down. I took another swallow and closed my eyes.

"Girls, don't you think it's time for bed?" Mr. McReddy said from the hallway. Corrie snatched the bottle and put it under her blanket. "We were just about to turn out the light, Dad."

"Okay, then. Sleep well, everyone." His footsteps sank away from the door.

"One more, for a nightcap," Corrie said, and passed the bottle back. I took another swig, and the hot-sour liquid raked my throat.

"I'm com-ing," Suzan whispered. Corrie hooted, then clapped a hand over her mouth.

I suddenly felt exhausted, as if my whole body was wrapped in stiff, wet blankets. I unzipped my sleeping bag and got in. Corrie climbed into her bed; Suzan and Michelle burrowed into their sleeping bags.

"G'night, you all," Corrie said.

"And let the bedbugs bite," Suzan said. "Just kidding."

Next to me, I could hear Michelle whispering into her pillow: "And God bless Mommy and Daddy and Kurt and Laurie and Grandpa Joseph and my gerbil, Puffy, and . . ."

I woke up with my stomach sizzling. My mouth and throat tasted like lemon rind, my head drummed, and my sleeping bag was clammy from sweat. I stood up shakily and stepped over the sleeping cocoons of Suzan and Michelle, making my way into the hall.

There were three doors besides ours; one of them had a band of light coming from underneath. Maybe the McReddys left a nightlight in the bathroom, the way we did at home. I stumbled toward that door, reached for the knob, and pulled.

"Vaneesa!" It was Mr. McReddy, sitting up in a single bed in a small room, a magazine open on his knees. I screamed. Then a different door opened, and there was Mrs. McReddy, tying her bathrobe and saying, "What is it? What's the matter?"

"I don't know—she just opened my door. Are you sick, Vaneessa?" I looked back and forth from one of them to the other, the lighted wedge of Mrs. McReddy's room, the stripes on her robe, Mr. McReddy's tiny eyes behind his glasses, all his shoes lined up neatly by his twin bed, and then I said, "I'm sorry," dropped my head, and threw up on the carpet between them.

My mom told me later that Mrs. McReddy went right to Corrie and Jenny's room while Mr. McReddy pointed me toward the bathroom. Mrs. McReddy saw the Wild Turkey bottle in the middle of the floor and shook Corrie until she woke up. Michelle cried, and Suzan pretended to be sound asleep until she heard Mr. McReddy say something about calling her father.

What I remember is tossing cold water on my face and tiptoeing into the hall, past the bedroom where both parents were yelling at once and Corrie was saying, "We didn't make her drink it. Nobody made anybody do anything!" I went quietly down the stairs, put on my jacket over the harlequin pajamas, and opened the sliding glass doors from the kitchen to the deck. Jenny was sitting at the picnic table, reading in the yellow-orange stain from the porch light.

I breathed in deeply, letting the air scrub sourness out of my mouth. "Hi, Jen," I said.

"You look awful."

"I threw up. Once in the hall, and once in the bathroom."

"It's okay," she said. "The first time Corrie made me drink that stuff, I tossed my dinner, too. Now I know better."

"She didn't make me drink it."

"Right. I was there, remember? Corrie's friends do whatever Corrie says—that is, as long as Suzan approves. And the ones who aren't really her friends but want to be—they do it twice as fast."

I felt my face get hot, and another wave of bitterness climbed into my mouth. I sat down next to Jen on the picnic bench and closed my eyes. When I opened them, the sky was still, the stars tiny rips in the night's black. If you stuck your finger in one and pulled, the whole fabric would tear apart.

"Want some gum?" Jen said. Before I could answer, she reached in the pocket of her robe, took out a piece of Wrigley's spearmint, and tore it in half.

"Sometimes I read out here all night," she said.

"Don't you get cold?" I was shivering already, the air scraping into the collar of my pajamas.

"Yeah, but it's better than being up there." She pointed at the second-story windows, patches of yellow with shapes flinching behind the shades. "With them. Especially her. Why do you like her so much? Why does everyone like her so much?"

"I don't know."

A car sped around the corner, tires screeching. The sound startled me, and I grabbed Jen's hand without thinking.

"Your hand's freezing." She rubbed both of hers over mine, sandwiching my fingers. In the orangey light, she looked haunted—wide, dark eyes, black hair, shadows slipping across her face—and beautiful. I tilted my head back.

"Look at the moon," I said. "Looks like a claw."

"Like a fingernail clipping."

"An apostrophe."

"Hey, that's good," Jen said. "A banana."

"A smile."

"A frown—if you turn the other way."

"An earring?"

"An ear," she said, and tugged on mine.

"A mouth," I said. Her fingers were cool and chapped, curtains that parted slightly, then rippled shut again, tickling my palm.

"Moon, June, balloon, harpoon," Jen said.

"Cartoon, saloon, pantaloon."

We were still holding hands when the kitchen door slid open and a voice said, "Jennifer Ann McReddy, get inside this instant."

I fell asleep on the living room couch while everyone was still yelling upstairs. In the morning, I poured myself some 7-Up and toasted a Pop-Tart. I knew it was against the McReddys' rules, but I didn't care. I was sitting on the front steps, reading the Sunday comics, when my mom drove up.

"Hi, honey. Heard you girls had a pretty exciting night," she said when I got in the car.

"I guess."

"You feeling better?"

"I think so." I kept sneaking glances at her while she drove. Had she and my dad been doing it in San Francisco? Did someone on the other side of the wall stay up and listen to them groaning and squeaking? Did they twist their bodies the way Suzan did on the carpet?

"Anything else you want to tell me about last night?"

"Nope."

"Okay. I think you'd better take it easy today. I'll make you some plain rice. I hope you've learned something from all this."

"Uh-huh . . . Mom, do you and Dad ever sleep in separate rooms?"

"Only if one of us is sick and doesn't want the other one to catch it. Why do you ask?"

"I don't know. Just wondering."

"Hmmm. Well, other than the unfortunate consequences of drinking Wild Turkey, did you have a good time?"

"I guess so. I mean, no, not really. I think I hate Corrie McReddy."

"Neesa! I'm surprised at you. Maybe you dislike her, or you strongly disagree with her, but you don't hate her."

"Okay, fine, I don't hate her."

"Good. That's good. I'm sure she doesn't hate you."

I closed my eyes then and let my body rock with the car's motion, side to side, side to side, until we were home.

I was never invited to the McReddys' house again. For a while, Corrie and Suzan followed me home from school, throwing pebbles at my ankles and calling, "Are you coming? Oh, ohhhh, are you *coming*, Neesa?" Michelle's parents took her out of our school and sent her to St. Catherine's. At the end of the year, a week or so before summer vacation, my mom told me the McReddys were getting a divorce.

"Why?" I said.

"I don't know, honey. I always thought they had a good marriage. A little formal, maybe, but solid. I guess you never really know what goes on in someone else's house."

That afternoon, I rode my bike over to the McReddys'. Jen was sitting on the porch with a book. Mr. McReddy's Datsun was packed and parked in the driveway. I walked my bike up the steps. "Can I sit down?"

"Sure." She shrugged.

"My mom told me your parents are getting a divorce. I'm really sorry."

"Yeah, well, whatever. Not like it's any big surprise. Corrie's gonna go live with my dad. I think they flipped a coin, and he won. So my mom gets stuck with me, and vice versa."

"Your mom's not so bad," I said.

"She's not really my mom," Jenny said. "You know that song 'Half Breed' that Cher sings? Well, I'm a half-breed. I'm part Indian. I know another language. My real parents gave me up for adoption, and these stupid jerks got me. You don't believe me, do you? But it's the truth."

It was almost dinnertime. Flags of pink falling across the sky, then ocean blue, then darker, moon rising.

"Looks like a cradle," I said, pointing up.

Jen shrugged. "If you say so."

"Don't you remember—Corrie's party, that horrible night, then afterward when we sat on the porch and said what the moon looked like?"

"I don't know what you're talking about."

"Come on, Jen, you've got to remember. We were making up rhymes. It was great."

Now she looked at me like I was a stranger. "I don't remember," she said. "I don't remember anything great in this house, ever." And she stood up with her book and went inside.

I biked home and told my mom I was going to take a bath. In the tub, I read the flowered booklet for the 107th time and tried to find all the parts it showed. I looked down between the strands of hair I was starting to get and separated the petals of skin; there was a thing like a bud that wasn't in the diagram.

I ran more hot water and added bubbles, then closed my eyes and sank in the tub up to my chin. Truth or dare, I thought. What is the true name for the part of me that's not even in the picture? Dare: Touch the bud between your legs. I did, and a small tingle, like a shock from the carpet, buzzed through me.

"Neesa, dinner's ready," my mom called. Through the closed door and the cloud of steam, the whispering bubbles and the tongues of water, her voice sounded far away. Anyway, I wasn't hungry. Secrets twisted inside me, shiny and frantic as new-caught fish.

Underneath

When Maddie Moran was ten years old, she had a friend with pigtails pale as egg whites, who vowed that, when she grew up, she would eat only albino vegetables. Ivory-colored eggplants, luminous golden beets, pearly fingers of asparagus. Maddie didn't understand, but she loved her friend's serious pink eyes.

"Won't you miss peas and carrots and tomatoes?" she asked.

"No. They're . . . noisy. They make my eyes hurt." Maddie's friend spread her fingers, ghost starfish, and covered her face.

"Look at me," Maddie commanded.

"I can't. You're too alive."

That's what they all said about Maddie, more or less. "Sit still, girl; stop hopping around like you got bees in your bloomers." "Don't ask so many darn questions; the Lord don't favor sassy tongues." Her mother put her to bed at night by laying a finger over her daughter's lips and whispering, "Do be quiet, Maddie."

She learned. Learned to say, "Yes, Father," and "No, thank you, ma'am," learned to contain the thoughts that burned her throat like ginger beer. Learned to sit with her legs crossed and to wash dishes so light waltzed off their rims.

But when no one was looking, Maddie buried her face in the mint bed until its bright tongues serrated her ears and cheeks, filled her nose with tiny stings of green. She stood naked after a bath, watching drops of water sluice off her warm skin, wander over her belly, lose themselves in the small nest of hair. She liked the smell of herself, even the rusty smear on her thighs once a month. Sometimes she dipped a finger in and tasted the blood, salt and copper on her tongue. Alive was a secret nobody knew.

Lyle Tanner owned the garage in town. Senior year, Maddie bought a pack of Wrigley's every day and chewed it in the parking lot so she could watch Lyle slide underneath a Chevy on the wheeled wooden board, ease back out like he'd been visiting another country, his mouth full of new language—*piston* and *spark, wheel bearing, clutch.*

He'd stand, wipe his hands on a turpentine rag. "Ma'am, that screechy noise you're starting to hear, like a cat with its paw stuck in a screen door? Well, your brake shoes are going. Soon it'll be metal on metal and the sound'll be like to break your bones. Best fix it now—you and the car'll be happier for it."

One day, he turned to Maddie. "If you need a job after graduation, I could use someone to do the books."

Maddie pushed both hands into her pockets. "I'm no good with figures. I want to do what you do." Lyle tipped his head like the whole world had suddenly got knocked fifteen degrees to the left and he had to compensate in order to see straight. He looked Maddie up and down.

"I think I got some coveralls would fit you."

Under the cars, it was greasy and quiet, black and warm. Lyle moved Maddie's hand from one part to the next, naming, explaining. The car was like a human body, he said, eating air and gasoline, belching little explosions into the cylinders so the pistons would pump up and down, camshaft connected to the crankshaft, all of it wrapped up in a tendon called the timing belt, which kept everything turning to the right beat.

Lyle was a big man—six foot one, solid as cedar—but his fingers were reedy, delicate. Maddie watched them unlock the bolt on the oil pan, drain its murky contents tenderly as letting blood.

At the end of the lesson, they crowded into the station's tiny bathroom and scrubbed with orange soap the consistency of winter molasses. The old mirror warped their faces into cartoons. Lyle stuck out his tongue. Maddie waggled her fingers in her ears. Then she stood on her toes and tilted her face up, pulled Lyle's chin down. He tasted of honeysuckle and hamburger, motor oil, mint.

"Please do that again," he said. "So I'll know I didn't make it up."

In a town where most folks were afraid to live too loud, Lyle and Maddie caused some talk. It wasn't just the twelve-year age difference, or Maddie working on the cars, or Lyle keeping the station open on Sundays, though that didn't land them in anyone's good graces. They'd be sprawled under a Dodge with a crotchety carburetor, church bells pealing a long way off, and watch the feet go by in their polished best, heels tapping disapproval on the station sidewalk.

What really fired folks up was their refusal to marry. "Never could see the sense in a preacher or a judge giving the A-okay to do what we're already doing," Lyle said. "Sorta like having a vote on whether the tomatoes ought to turn red on the vine."

As soon as Maddie turned eighteen, she moved into Lyle's neat, cramped house next to the garage. Everything she owned—a bentwood rocker, her great-grandma's rose-pattern dishes, a box of dahlia bulbs—fit in the trunk of a car. They worked at the station Sunday through Thursday; weekends, they drove out to McConaghey Lake and watched the water steep from aquamarine to khaki to slate to black.

"That cloud," Maddie said, pointing. "Looks exactly like Pastor Dave's wife, right after she's been to the beauty parlor for a permanent wave, don't you think?" Lyle laughed so hard, he wet his pants and had to drive home wearing a towel knotted around his waist like a sarong. Neighbors stared and coughed into their shirtsleeves when he sauntered out of the car. Lyle was like Adam before the Fall; no one had told him to be ashamed of himself. And Maddie would have been Eve, hungry to know every forbidden corner of the garden.

Lyle told her how birds sang the perimeters of their territory and showed her the painted tongues of orchids, how each flower was perfectly made to be a landing pad for the particular kind of insect that loved its pollen. He pointed out how it makes sense that fruit is laxative, so animals will drop the seeds in their scat.

"See, everything is wired to live," he said. "Things just can't help growing, finding a way. Plant a sunflower in the basement and it will rotate with the sun, even if there's only a tiny bit of light coming through a crack in the cement."

Maddie taught him love. The bone-tingling savor of running a tongue ever so lightly over the other's gums. Gums: Who would have thought? She washed their sheets with peppermint, ground cinnamon into the coffee, brought a whole steamed artichoke to bed and showed Lyle the tender heart in its fist of leaves. He wept when he tasted the first bite.

"I love you, Maddie," he said, moving his fingers softly, everywhere. In a town buttoned up to its collarbone, their bodies were open vaults, gulping pleasure, leaking it back into the world. When Maddie sat up in bed, looking through the window at the full moon corked in an ink-bottle sky, and tears slipped down her face, Lyle simply took her hand and said, "I know, I know."

One night, wind spanked the house; hard rain stippled the windows. Maddie slid chocolate chip cookies into the oven while Lyle drove out for a quart of milk. He looked like a hydrant in his orange slicker. Twenty minutes later, the cookies were done. Forty-five minutes, and Lyle still wasn't back. An hour, an hour and twenty, two hours and ten. Then the doorbell rang, and a police officer with his hat in his hand called Maddie "ma'am" for the first time in her life.

She stood there silent while he talked: "Low visibility . . . slick roadway . . . maximum impact . . . dead on arrival." In the kitchen, the cookies were still warm. Maddie grabbed handfuls of them, squeezed her fists until butter greased her palms and chopped nuts oozed between her fingers. Then, sobbing, she flattened her hands to the walls, leaving graffiti of chocolate and tears.

She hoped she would wake up dead. But morning came with the same pink-ribbon sunrise as every other day in history, birds calling out their boundaries, spiders showing off a night's worth of spinning, their webs spangled with dew. It was March, and already the tulips were coming up, cheerful, resilient shoots of green. She hated them. The world teemed with sound and color, smell and texture. Maddie dressed in gray, drew the shades, ate dry toast and plain tea.

"Of course you feel sad, dear," the pastor's wife said through the storm door. "But none of us can know God's plan. 'To every thing there is a season,' you know; that's what the Good Book says. 'A time to be born, and a time to—' "

Maddie slammed the door. Sadness wasn't a thing she felt, the way you stretch out your hand to feel for rain; it's what she *was*. Every inch of her body stung; her hair ached and her toenails bit into her toes. When she took a walk, it seemed outrageous that the grass didn't die under her feet, that the tabby brushing by her leg didn't turn immediately to ash. She longed to leave a wet streak of grief in the world, like a snail.

Neighbors delivered casseroles to the front porch; Maddie thanked them and scooped the food directly into the garbage. Now there were nine clean casserole dishes, one for each day since Lyle's death, on her dining room table. She could smash them, one by one, but the sound of breaking china would be too festive. Instead, she plunged the rose-pattern cups into a sink of greasy dishwater. Each one made a sucking sound as it filled, a last gasp before drowning. Maddie scrubbed the Teflon skillet with a pad that bled powdery blue soap. It felt good to hurt the smooth coating, leave a tattoo of rage.

And that's when she felt it for the first time. A pinch that pulled her back into her own body. She knew it was impossible; it had been conceived only two weeks ago, five days before Lyle died, but she could feel it anyway, little bead of determination burrowing into the bloody down of her uterus, bound to get what it needed from this world. Tiny sexless fish, no larger than a question mark on a page of newsprint. Maddie put her hand to her belly, fingers splayed like a star.

BLOOD

Anatomies

There are 206 bones in the adult human skeleton, and the flight from Baltimore to Miami took two hours and fifty-seven minutes. That meant seventy bones an hour, one bone every fifty-one seconds.

Mia had a system. First, she stared at the textbook, memorizing the bone's shape and curvature, the hollows in its knobbed end. She imagined the name imprinted across its length. Then she covered the name with her hand and repeated it to herself, like a mantra. Occipital, parietal, frontal. Sphenoid, ethmoid.

She liked their Latin melody and the lacy pattern they made, delicately hinged together, floating through the pages of *Gray's Anatomy.* Some people found the skeleton diagrams eerie, but they made Mia think of hand-tooled birdcages, an art form at once pure and functional. Each bone nestled into the adjacent one, everything in its place.

Mia knew that once she arrived in Miami, there would be no time to memorize bones. She would need to make phone calls, knock on doors, scout the neighborhood, calm her grandfather. He'd woken her at 2:00 A.M., Spanish streaming hysterically over the long-distance line. Something about her grandmother Lena. A trip to the ice-cream store? Or maybe it was to buy oranges.

"*Mas despacio*," she'd pleaded. "Slowly. *Por favor, Abuelo, en ingles.*" Finally, she was able to understand that Lena had taken a walk with the dog to get ice cream the night before. She'd left Alberto watching television. When he woke up, it was 1:00 A.M. and neither Lena nor the dog was home.

"Have you called the police?" Mia asked, and another torrent of Spanish splashed over the phone.

"*La policía*? They don't help. They have holes in their hearts." Then Alberto took a few gulps of air, and wept.

Mia let him cry a minute. She should have known better. One of her earliest memories of Miami was walking with Alberto through Coral Gables. She was making up a story about elves who lived in banyan trees when he suddenly clutched her arm and dragged her into a stranger's driveway. The two crouched there while a police officer strolled past. Her grandfather's shoulder quivered under his thin shirt. Mia, at seven, was unable to explain that things were different here, that this was America, that they were safe.

Alberto's family were Sephardim who'd fled Madrid in the late 1400s, just in time. They lived in Belgium, in the Netherlands, and finally in Austria, until the brown-shirted soldiers came. Alberto decided then to insert an ocean in his family's history. He took his beautiful, stubborn bride to Argentina, where the language reminded him of Ladino lullabies.

Mia's father, Fredo, was born three months after their arrival in

Buenos Aires. He was a writer who later married a photographer. Together, they produced three illustrated books about Argentina's rural poor—and Mia, their only child.

They all lived together: Mia and her parents, Lena and Alberto. Mia remembered a yard full of white zephyr flowers and a house spilling with cigarette smoke, amber liquid in glasses, and constant, agitated conversation. And this: When she was six, a new police— Spanish-speaking, this time—came to the house on a Tuesday evening and put handcuffs on her father right before dessert.

"*Ha desaparecido,*" she heard Alberto say through tears.

"*En* Argentina, *sí. Pero en* Miami, *no. Personas* don't disappear," she told him. "*Tienes que llamar a la policía*, okay? You have to call. I'll take the first flight I can get after classes tomorrow."

It was dusk now, and the plane was filling. A cluster of Girl Scouts in matching kneesocks. A tall man talking to another man, nodding and saying, "Absolutely. Yes, absolutely." Mia flipped to the next chapter in her book, the one after bones. The clean, spare skeleton was dressed in what looked like rare steaks, a weft of muscle, tendons, and ligaments, overlapping strands of white and red.

Mia was going to turn thirty-three next week, and her grandmother was missing. Maybe she was too old to be in medical school, too old to be reminded daily of how much she didn't know.

I want the window," said a voice. Mia looked up. A little boy in green overalls stood in the aisle, frowning at her. His skin was satin black, his eyes full of reproach. Another voice, breathless, came from a few rows ahead.

"No, Taylor, you can't sit by the window, because I have to keep my foot in the aisle, and you have to sit next to me." While Mia watched, Taylor's face transformed like a fast-motion film of a crying child, his eyes spilling with tears, his chin trembling.

A woman hobbled into view. Her light red hair was escaping from a ponytail. She'd slung bags over both shoulders and had a crutch under one arm. Her left foot was bound in a knee-high cast and a blue cloth slipper. "I don't mind sitting in the middle," Mia said, and stood up so Taylor could squeeze by. The woman sat down in the aisle seat, stuck her foot out diagonally, and extended her hand. "I'm Estelle. This is Taylor. And you're a life saver."

The plane began to climb. "Up, up, up, up," Taylor reported. As soon as they'd leveled, he lost interest in the view and turned to Mia.

"I'm Taylor, and that's my mom, but she's not my birth mom. My birth mom died."

"Oh," Mia said.

"Do you have a birth mom?"

"Yes, I do—I mean, I think so. Actually, Taylor, I haven't seen her for a long, long time."

The night Mia's father was arrested, Alberto shoved the family's clothes into three suitcases. They would go to Miami, he said. But at the last minute, Mia's mother sat on the couch and clutched a pillow to her chest. You choose, she told her daughter. Stay or go. Whatever you want. Mia had learned in school that America was the place where people went to stay forever. Alberto and Lena held out their arms, and she ran.

On the boat, Mia would not walk on the deck, but lay in her bunk day and night, hugging the covers. She wept and screamed, refused to eat. By the time they arrived in Miami, her body felt empty of moisture. Her eyelashes stuck together; her skin was mapped with white salty lines.

Alberto and Lena had to hold her steady as they came off the boat. Mia swayed a little, turned her face up to the Miami heat, and drank it in. She wriggled out of her grandparents' arms and walked into perfumes of bougainvillea, past houses bleached bone white. She did not look back.

For a long time, Lena sent a letter to Buenos Aires every week. "Do you have anything to add?" she'd ask Mia, and Mia would shake her head no. Still, she ran to the mailbox each afternoon, looking for a thin blue envelope with familiar script. Eventually, every piece of mail came back—slit open, resealed with cellophane tape, and stamped "No such person." After a while, Mia couldn't picture her mother's handwriting, or remember her laugh. Even her face blurred, and whole pieces of Mia's childhood went with it, like flesh withering away from the bone.

Mia turned back to *Gray's Anatomy*. Humerus, ulna, radius, carpus. Long fingers like jointed cigarettes. But she was seeing Lena's hands, cinnamon brown and crinkled, her nails polished red, with two fistfuls of turquoise rings. Mia remembered lying in the garden, watching those hands prune a jacaranda bush, the turquoise lumps flashing like eyes among the lavender flowers. Her own hands were paler, less dramatic even when she fussed over her nails, and she had no touch for growing things. Even her houseplants died. Maybe she would have better luck with people.

"I'm hungry," Taylor announced. Estelle reached into one of the tote bags and produced a plastic sack of what looked to Mia like miniature oranges.

"Kumquats," she said. "He loves them. We were in the market one day—he couldn't have been more than two—and he pointed and said, 'I want those.' "And then she shrugged, as if to say, Who knows where kids really come from? A quick shrug, and a smile that meant she'd long ago stopped asking that question, had come to understand child rearing as a daily series of gifts and shocks.

"What are you reading?" Taylor pulled on Mia's sleeve.

"A medical book. About bones. I'm going to be a doctor, so I have to learn the names of all the bones. I've done fourteen of them. I have a hundred and ninety-two to go."

"A doctor fixed my mom's foot, but she still has to wear that slipper," he said.

"Yeah, it can take a long time to heal."

Taylor looked out the window again. "Do doctors ever cut people's hearts?"

"Ummm . . . well, sometimes. If their heart has a disease."

This conversation was moving into shaky territory, out of her field of expertise. Cardiology was at least a semester away.

"Hearts mean 'I love you,' right?"

Now Mia was really getting concerned. She glanced at Estelle for help, but her eyes were closed, her plaster-bound foot stuck into the aisle.

"Right," she told Taylor emphatically.

"So if you cut somebody's heart, do all the 'I love yous' fall out?"

"That's a good question, Taylor. I think the doctors just put them back in and sew up the hole."

The child looked at her for a moment, and she felt as if she were under the scrutiny of a resident, being grilled about a chapter she'd somehow failed to study.

"I don't think so," he said slowly. "I think some of the 'I love yous' get lost. They fall down to your toes and come out the holes in your socks. And then you get sad because your heart isn't so red anymore, more like pinkish."

Mia closed her book. "Taylor, how about another kumquat?" She took one from the bag on Estelle's lap and handed it over.

Maybe, she reasoned, Lena had simply gotten confused. She'd been losing her sight gradually in the past five years, gardening by scent and touch and memory, feeling her way across the backyard of their small bungalow. Mia asked her once what it was like to go blind, and Lena paused for a long time on the phone. "*El sol desaparece.*" The sun disappears.

On Mia's last visit to Miami, she had gone to the beach at five o'clock one morning, when it was empty, and ran for ten minutes with her eyes closed. She'd thought each second would grow easier, that she'd be nudged along by the certainty of having planted her last step safely on the ground.

But it was the opposite. The longer she ran, the shakier she felt. Each scuff of foot to sand was a miracle, and the next one a dare.

She flew back to Baltimore after that visit and made a decision. She would enroll in medical school. She would memorize organs and muscles, glandular secretions and diseases of the ear, everything that could possibly go wrong with a human body. She would keep her eyes open. She would not miss a thing.

The night before she started classes, she dreamed about standing in a garden of jacaranda. Her nails were long and polished red. When she turned her hands over, she saw that a seed had been planted in each calcium cup. Vines dangled from her fingers. They trailed over the entire world and took root in all the places her family had ever lived.

"In fifteen minutes, we will be arriving at Miami International Airport," said a tinny voice. Taylor had fallen asleep, his body half-slumped over Mia's right knee. The plane angled down, and Mia put a hand on his shoulder to steady him. Then—she couldn't help it—she pressed her fingers into the soft dark skin near his collar. Her hands massaged lightly, working over the small shoulder. Clavicle. Scapula. Humerus.

Mia turned to her left, as if to reassure Estelle, to say, "Your son is whole." But Estelle was asleep, her face softened in a pout identical to Taylor's. The bag of kumquats was still in her lap.

Mia took one out and examined it. Smaller than a golf ball, slightly pocked skin. She put it in her mouth and bit down. A bitter taste rode her tongue; then a bright perfume followed. She chewed the pulpy mass, sucking the juice, at once sweet and stinging.

And then she remembered what Alberto was saying about oranges on the phone last night. "*Mi media naranja*," he'd sobbed. My half orange. He meant Lena. It was an endearment, like "better half" in English. Mia's mother used to call her father that, her voice soft as they bent together over a page of typescript.

Mia leaned across Taylor's back and looked out the window. The earth reared toward them. Lights blinked across the landscape, and it seemed for a moment that they spelled out a message, a kind of illuminated braille. Where Lena was, perhaps. How people got holes in their hearts, and whether there was any hope of repair. If she could only hover at that precise altitude, in the clear, dark night, she could read what the lights had to tell her.

But the plane did not stop. It dived steeply toward Miami. The lights grew brighter, streaming all over the ground. In their midst, a gash of tarmac. At the end of it would be Alberto.

Mia imagined walking off the plane into his frightened gaze. The tears would seep from their faces like nectar from an orange chopped in two. She knew how they would clasp each other hard, how their bones—scapula, clavicle, radius, ulna—would take the shock.

Do Not Attempt to Climb Out

It felt, Omar thought, like a domino stuck in the throat. A double twelve, black as a shingle, crazy with dots, corners wedged up against the soft tissue. Going nowhere. Not up, not down.

If Omar were the praying type, this would be the moment to drop to his haunches on the fake marble floor, whisper a fevered entreaty: Oh dear Lord, make this elevator *move*. But Omar had not prayed in years, and he figured God was not the sort to answer requests from relative strangers: Hey, remember me, the one You baptized in Greenville, South Carolina, oh, about forty-seven years ago? Little brown baby in a christening dress look like a lace hankie? Omar figured God was no better or worse, no more generous or less jealous, than your average next-door neighbor. You had to keep up some kind of passing acquaintance, make a habit of remarking about the dahlias or the Yankees, if you expected any kind of help when a hurricane spit your storm gutters to the ground.

If Sissy were here, no doubt they'd be knee-deep in prayer by now, her daisy of a voice calling out the troops: God, Mary, Jesus, Joseph, and all the saintly cousins. Omar would be lost in the crowd, arms pinned, useless, to his sides. A pillar of her church, that's what his sister was, and Omar never heard the phrase without thinking of the chalky columns holding up the balcony of First Avenue Baptist back home. Even as a girl, Sissy had behaved as if all that weight, all the church's wriggling latecomers, were her personal responsibility.

It had never made much sense to Omar why the preachers were all men, when piety came more naturally to women. The calling out, the bargaining, the songs, the tears. His father stayed home on Sunday mornings, playing solitaire, while Momma hustled Omar and Sissy into stiff clothes and clean socks and walked them up First Avenue to sit for hours in a church so hot the hymnals wilted and a tenor once passed out during his solo. Back home, his father drank Jim Beam from a jelly glass and plucked at dog-eared aces.

The only part of church Omar loved was afterward, when they trudged home and sat down for Momma's meal. Chicken so tender it melted off the bone, greens babied with fatback and burnt nubs of bacon, corn bread that gave a kiss of steam when he broke it in two. They held hands around the table, bowed heads, and his father said simply, "Thank you." For a moment, they were all in agreement: The food was good.

So, no, Omar would not be calling on God or Jesus to get him out of this one. He guessed he would not be pushing that red button, either—the one next to the sign that said HELP WILL ARRIVE SOON. DO NOT ATTEMPT TO CLIMB OUT. It was 3:00 A.M., and he was not supposed to be in this elevator. He'd been polishing the lobby when he got the urge to go up. There was

83

a restaurant on the thirty-fifth floor, a revolving bar with a hundred eyes out to the city. Once, while cleaning, Omar had found a receipt in the stairwell: two brandies and a chocolate mousse, come to thirty-one dollars. How much would they charge for a glass of water and a long stare out the window? The restaurant was closed now—last call was 2:00 A.M.—but Omar just wanted to feel that cool glass on his cheek, see what there was to see.

He parked the polishing machine against the wall and gave it a stern look: You stay put, now. He pressed the button for the center elevator. The doors slipped open, he stepped inside, and they glided shut. All around the elevator was a waist-high brass rail; above that, the walls were papered beige. Omar pressed the button marked 35, and the elevator began to sing its way up, one soft note for each floor.

Just past the seventeenth floor, something happened: A hitch, a shudder, and then everything stood still. Omar pressed 35 again. Nothing. He pressed 18. He pressed M for mezzanine, L for lobby, B for basement; finally, he pressed them all, punching rapidly up one column and down the other, then at random, as if there were a combination—six, twenty-three, eleven, four, perhaps—that would deliver him. The elevator locked in the long throat of the building. His mouth dry as ash. Omar dug both his sweating, shaking hands into his pockets.

His father used to say a man had to play the cards he was dealt. But what if the dealer was crooked, or the cards were marked? What if your prayers never went further than the box you were stuck in? He should have stayed put. That's what the contract said: Scrub the lobby and the ground-floor rest rooms; polish the bronze fittings; wipe smudges from the revolving glass. The upstairs offices hired their own cleaners. Omar never needed to leave the ground. It wasn't a bad job, not when you added in the side benefits: an occasional fountain pen in a corner, dollar bills wadded next to the john, once a silver money clip with the initials LJR. It wasn't quite stealing, because the objects were already lost. Omar just wasn't helping them get found.

He pulled one hand from his pocket to check his watch. Damn. In five hours and forty minutes, Sissy would come by his house, as she did every Sunday morning, to see if he wanted to go to church. "Omah," she'd say—even up north, after all these years, she said his name with a melting consonant at the end, the way Momma had. "Omah, will you be greetin' the Lord with me this mornin'?"

"No, I don't suppose I will," he said every time, and the look on Sissy's face was exactly the same as his father's when the last solitaire card failed to connect, when the promise of a winning game folded up and died.

It took years for Omar's father to drink himself into a reeking yellow death. Momma had tended him without a word. After that, she seemed to go gray—not just her hair but *all* of her, overnight—and died three years later. Sissy went off to Philadelphia to study social working. Omar drove her up, then found his way out to Brandywine Raceway and laid his small inheritance on a filly named Liberty Belle. She was nosing out the number-one horse when she stumbled in the stretch, and there it went. That's when Omar cried. Not at the brown spittle on his father's chin, not when they slid Momma's box into its slot in the earth. He wept like a baby when Liberty Belle lost her footing and crumpled to the track.

Omar grabbed the brass rail and held it with both hands. If he got out of this elevator alive and without losing his job, maybe he would say yes to Sissy one of these Sundays. Or maybe he would get lucky on the slots and take Sissy up for a drink on the thirty-fifth floor. He would stretch out one arm toward the city as if he'd made it himself. He'd pay for their drinks, peeling bills from a money clip that bore his own initials.

No. Sissy was afraid of heights. And it could be, from the thirty-fifth floor, that a person missed more than he saw. So much would be invisible up there: no bare foot poked out from a blanket on Broad Street, no lady feeding her kid from a Dumpster behind DiNardo's, no old man crying in another language on the corner bench in Rittenhouse Square. The bar would turn slowly over tangled-up neon, a quilt of lighted and dark windows, and you would not hear a soul cheating or fighting or loving or dying. Just the pure ring of glass on glass, and the honey burn of brandy on your tongue.

Omar felt as if he were about to sneeze. Stinging pinch at the base of his nose, wet tickle around his eyes, rectangular lump pressing the sides of his throat. Maybe his father had prayed each Sunday—Oh Jesus, please just this once—for the solitaire cards to turn out right. Maybe his mother had laid her half-dollar in the collection plate, crossed her fingers, and gambled it would come back tenfold. If God could just get him out of here in time for Sissy to come by and say his name soft as a biscuit: Omah, will you be greetin' the Lord with me?

The icy lights overhead flickered and went out, and Omar dropped to the floor, sobbing into his palms. The walls trembled, the elevator floated for one sickening second between nothing and nowhere, and then it began to move, though Omar could not tell whether he was sinking or rising.

Local Currency

Six nights a week, Medio Cabrales de Sanchez sprayed himself the color of money from eyebrow to ankle, propped a sign in the amphitheater near the Miami marina, and performed every hour on the hour from 7:00 P.M. until the crowds went home.

"Mommy, look, there's Mr. Silver," he heard children say as he walked past boutique windows, juice bars, restaurants where tourists ordered Cuban black beans from waitresses named Traci. Sometimes his own reflection in the plate glass startled him: silver, from the crown of his slicked-back ponytail to the ends of his pewter toes. Silver hair spray, metallic makeup, slate-colored bodysuit, and shorts made of a thin, shiny cloth normally used for parachutes. He had searched all over Miami for silver shoes in a size twelve until a drag queen friend suggested he spray-paint a pair of secondhand sandals.

"All you need on those are some little silver wings—then you can get a job as the FTD flower boy," Chris said once, watching Medio dress for work. Medio did not find this amusing. In the mirror, his body looked like a metal outdoor statue, smooth and cool to the touch. "Sorry. Must be one of those cultural-reference jokes," Chris said, and turned back to his canvas.

The act Medio performed thirty or so times a week was not exactly dance, although he moved with imagination and grace; not exactly mime, though it was true he did not speak; not political enough to qualify as the sort of performance art Chris's friends praised at cocktail parties. Medio set a spray-painted top hat and a battery-operated boom box on the ground, played salsa, ragtime, and jazz tapes with plenty of percussion, and then simply moved to them.

He matched his gestures to the music—sometimes staccato and robotic, sometimes silky and unbroken. He had a particular talent for freezing one part of his body while exercising another, and the crowds rewarded him with rounds of applause when he held one arm straight out while the rest of his body shuddered and twisted as if caught in a tropical storm.

For the finale, he would stand motionless for a minute, then allow his body to ripple as if seized by electricity, starting with a rapid blinking of his eyes, then a quick twitching of the lips and chin, all the way down to whirling pelvis, thrumming knees, toes that rapped a rhythm on the flats of his shoes. Afterward, in the storm of applause, he acknowledged each member of the audience with his eyes, starting and ending, always, with the children. He did not bow or smile, just inclined his head slightly as his glance moved from one face to the next.

The children stared back without apology. But Mr. Silver's refusal to break character seemed to unnerve the adults; he often watched mothers and fathers put a protective hand on their children's shoulders, tug lightly on their arms, and promise ice-cream sundaes in an effort to break the spell. The children wriggled from their parents' grasp, their thin arms waving in the air like sea plants.

"How did you learn to dance like that?"

"Are you a robot?"

"Do you take off your makeup before you go to bed?"

And, from the adolescent, bolder ones: "Are you silver *everywhere*?" asked with a knowledgeable snicker.

By way of answering, Mr. Silver handed out a photocopied sheet titled "Common Questions about Mr. Silver," and brief typed responses. This had been Chris's idea—one more of his efforts to teach Medio that art also required sound marketing. The sheet was good publicity, but it didn't stop the flow of questions, new ones each night, everyone trying to get behind Mr. Silver's impassive face.

"Are you related to the Tin Man in *The Wizard of Oz*?"

"How long does it take you to get that stuff on?"

"Are your brothers and sisters silver, too?"

The questions hung in the thick Miami night while Mr. Silver hit the rewind button on his tape deck, sipped at a can of Dr. Pepper, and used a damp sponge with a tin of metallic body paint to touch up any spots where his skin was starting to show through.

When friends asked Medio and Chris how they had met, they winked lasciviously and said, "In the men's room at the marina"—a place the Miami vice cops were constantly targeting as a "site of known homosexual activity." Both men were in the bathroom that August evening for perfectly practical reasons: Medio to add a bit more hair spray to his ponytail and Chris, who did chalk caricatures of tourists, to wash his hands.

They exchanged nods in the warped mirrors over the sinks, and Chris immediately got so nervous that he reached to slick back his hair before his hands were clean, streaking his forehead orange and purple. Medio, even though he was still in costume, broke into a smile.

"I've seen you . . . um, do your act," Chris said. "You move very well."

Medio blushed under his makeup. "I've seen you, too. The drawings, yes?"

"Oh, those." Chris made a face. "Art for the masses. Not much challenge, but at five dollars a pop, at least it pays the rent. I do real art, too—charcoal and oils. I'd like to paint you sometime—without the silver stuff." He reddened at his own suggestion. "I mean, you could wear regular clothes. You could just be yourself."

"Yeah, okay," Medio said. They traded phone numbers and shook hands chastely. When Chris went back to his easel, he noticed nickel-colored streaks across his palm.

Later, one of the oil paintings of Medio—sans silver, with clothes—was among the work a Coconut Grove gallery owner liked. Chris's first solo show got raves in the local press as "the penetrating vision of a young artist who sees beyond the borders of his own culture," and he ceremoniously dumped his colored chalk in the trash.

Medio performed every night but Monday. When he came home after midnight, he nudged Chris under the blanket, then turned over his hat so that coins and bills rained onto the bed. Together, they stacked the quarters and dimes, snapped creases out of the dollars, yelped when they came across an occasional five- or ten-dollar bill. Then Chris rolled back to sleep while Medio made careful note of his tips in a ledger, subtracting the twenty dollars he would send back to Piste.

For three years, he had been sending money orders home each Friday, with notes he block-printed in Spanish on sheets of notebook paper. At first, they were terse and honest: "I am trying to find a place to live. Miami is crowded, but many people speak Spanish. I might work cleaning in an office. As soon as I get some money, I will send it." After a few months, when his situation had not changed, he began to lie, just a little: He'd been noticed by the boss of the offices, who wanted to promote him. He'd found an apartment in a building with a pool. He'd met a nice girl, pretty; her name was Angela. As soon as he paid his next month's rent, he would send money.

The words were just words, Medio thought. What mattered was the money order his mother and brothers would clutch in their hands, money to buy masa and milk, money to pay the landlord when he came around with his sticky palm and his excuses for why, after eight years, the roof still leaked.

If Mr. Silver could earn enough money, he would buy his family a house in Playa del Carmen. No, he would move them all here and get a big apartment on a boulevard lined with trees, in a building with glass doors and a man to question your guests before they went upstairs. Money meant everything. Enough of it, and a mother never had to stretch the same pound of rice into six days' worth of dinner. Not enough, and she would thrash in her sleep, dreaming of scarcity.

The day Helena de Sanchez told her oldest son she was pregnant, she buried her face in her scarf while she whispered the words.

"Who?" Medio asked, anger scalding the roof of his mouth. "If anyone hurt you, I'll kill him." His mother shook her head, sobbing. "Don't tell your brothers. Not yet. Not until I've decided what to do."

Medio knew she couldn't mean abortion—not for a forty-three-year-old Catholic woman in a tiny Yucatán town. Even if she knew where to get one in secret, they could never afford the bribe. Helena choked her tears back, then said, "I think I'm going to give it away. All the time, there are Americans here, coming into town to see the ruins. I'll go to Chichén Itzá and talk to people from the tour buses. I'll know when I've found the right ones."

"No!" Medio stamped his foot, grabbed his mother's hands and shook them. "I won't have it. We'll take care of her—or him." Already he was imagining a sister. She would be the only girl in a family of five boys. He would show her how to plant a garden; he would plait her hair and bandage her knees when she fell, teach her to read. "Mami, you can't give it away."

His mother crossed her arms over her belly. "My baby. I decide. I decide for my children who are already here. This is final."

They did not speak about it again—not when Helena vomited in the dust each morning outside the pigpen, not as she began to groan at night with the baby's weight. Not when she brought home a brown-haired young couple one day and introduced them to Medio as "Sally and Bruce from Miami." The day after the baby was born, Sally and Bruce knocked softly on the door, and Medio took them into his mother's room. "Are you sure?" he asked Helena.

"Yes, yes." She handed the infant to Sally and turned her face to the wall. "Her name is Aureo. It means 'golden,'" she said in a thick voice. "Aureo," Sally repeated, and her lips touched the baby's forehead. "Sweet Aureo."

Bruce left a thick envelope of cash and a bag of groceries on the table. Medio never looked to see how much money it was. Before the couple left, they stood in the kitchen, shifting their feet around on the cracked linoleum. Sally held the baby close, cooing to her in a singsong. Bruce had tears in his eyes.

"Please tell your mother," he started, then had to stop and wipe his nose with the corner of a diaper. "We've wanted so much . . . for so long . . . I promise we'll be very good parents. She'll have a happy life. We'll tell her about"—and he gestured around the room— "where she came from. About her brothers. Thank you." Sally looked up from the baby, her green eyes full, and nodded at Medio. The baby sucked greedily on Sally's index finger.

Medio's entire body felt frozen, except for his eyes, which moved over every inch of his sister's tiny face.

When Helena was well enough to get out of bed, she made a little shrine for the baby, with a Virgin Mary statue, a rosary, and some sage. With the money Bruce left, she bought chickens and fabric for new clothes for the boys, seeds for the garden, two little spades so she would not have to dig with rocks. Medio's brothers strutted in their new shirts, teased the chickens, and helped in the garden only when they were forced. They never talked about the baby.

But she came in Medio's dreams, with her huge chocolate-colored eyes and damp fringe of black hair. In his dreams, the baby drifted alone on a boat in the middle of a choppy sea, or teetered on the windowsill of a tall building, or toddled into a street busy with cars. He would try to run toward her, shout a warning, but his voice was choked and his legs so heavy, prisoners of the cruel gravity of dreams. He'd wake up slick with sweat, his heart knocking.

At first, the dreams came only once in a while, then once a week, finally almost every night. Medio stayed awake as long as he could, trying to fend off the nightmares. As soon as he edged into sleep, his baby sister's face would appear, always balanced on the cusp of danger, always impossible to reach. Medio thought his head would split from worry. He stopped eating, couldn't work. All day long, his mind spun with dizzying thoughts and images: his sister, Miami, so far away.

"Mami, I have to go there," he said finally. "I'll get a job. I'll send money home; it will be okay. The boys are old enough. They can help you." He touched her cheek, tried to coax a smile. "You know what they say, that the streets of Miami are paved with gold."

"Go," she said, and gave him a little push. "If you have to, go."

After three months of sleeping in parks, eating scraps, and begging, Medio wandered the marina one night and got the idea for Mr. Silver. He watched a man do obvious, amateurish magic tricks, pulling colored scarves out of his sleeves, retrieving quarters from children's ears. He watched the adults throw money in a hat; he saw children tug their parents away from shopping and eating to the circle where the magician performed. The city was huge; he could not possibly walk every street in search of his sister. But he could be a magnet, make the children come to him.

In Medio's first months with Chris, the nightmares subsided. After noting his tips in the ledger each night, after a forty-five minute shower to remove the hair spray and stage paint and makeup, he climbed into bed and wrapped one arm around his lover's chest. "You know what they call us in Spanish?" he whispered. "*Mariposas*. Butterflies." His groin filled then with a sensation like small wings, and the two rolled toward each other, mouths hunting in the dark until they met.

Medio's dreams afterward were blinding and deep; it was only in the morning, when light put corners back on the objects in the room, that his body stiffened again and he could not tolerate Chris's touch. Sometimes there were silvery traces on the pillows, from a place Medio had neglected to wash, and Chris used to joke, "Hey, look, it's the silver lining in our clouds."

"Looks like tarnish," Medio muttered, then got up to make coffee. While it brewed, he would write home: "Dear Mami, I am working for a rich man as his gardener and cook. He pays me cash, no taxes, and I have my own room with a view of the ocean. My girlfriend is studying to be a teacher. When she is finished, we will get married." He wrote words that would make his mother smile and press the paper to her chest, over her heart, details of a life she could imagine. He folded the letter carefully, tucked in a money order for $20, and sealed the envelope.

A New York gallery wanted to show some of Chris's work, the oils of Medio and some of the charcoal sketches that had preceded them. At first, Medio said no—he didn't like the idea of his image hanging in a place so far away—but then he thought of all the people who might see it. Maybe one of them would notice a resemblance, would see that the model's eyes were just like those of a little girl they knew, a little girl named Aureo who lived in Miami with her parents, Sally and Bruce.

"Yes, fine, send them, I don't care," Medio said. Chris talked about New York more and more lately. That's where the real artists were, he said. In New York, they could rent a loft; they could go to the Metropolitan Museum of Art and eat linguine at 2:00 A.M. in Little Italy.

"Come on—it'll be an adventure. You could go to school, study dance. You're twenty-four years old—you can't be Mr. Silver all your life."

Medio pulled his hair tight into an elastic band and shook the aerosol can of silver spray. "My work is here, my audience. It's too cold in New York to dance outside. Anyway, I'd probably be arrested, or mugged. The paintings can go, but not me. This is final."

Chris grabbed his portfolio and left, slamming the door so hard, the bathroom mirror shook in its frame. In it, Medio watched his eyes redden, his face turn ruddy. Quickly, he covered the skin with a thick layer of metallic base.

That night, when Medio went into the bedroom, ready to empty his hat over Chris's sleeping body, he saw that the blankets were still pulled taut. There was a note on the pillow: "Went to a play with Leslie and Kama. Then a party at their house. Join us if you want." Kama and Leslie lived just a few blocks away. A party: Why not? He couldn't remember the last time he and Chris had had fun with other people. Medio showered quickly, not bothering to wash his hair, then changed clothes and walked over.

The party had wound down; it was only Leslie, Kama, and Chris sitting around a plate of crackers and grapes. Leslie hugged him at the door. "Hey, Medio, it's been so long. Come on in. But I'm warning you—it's the middle of a major discussion." From the hall, he could see Kama talking with her hands, the rocking chair swinging back and forth with the force of her speech. Chris was stretched out on the rug, his shoes off, and Medio suddenly wanted to lie down next to him, peel off his clothes, let Chris rub his muscles into butter.

"So if the lawyer actually shows up, and the court system—which is totally backward—doesn't make a mess of things, it should take three weeks or so for all the paperwork to go through," Kama was saying. "I'll fly down first; then Leslie will come to help me get the baby home. We're terrified, of course, but totally ready for this. And we're going to have a naming ceremony sometime, so keep your calendars open."

Medio's stomach tipped then, and the room began to buzz. Chris sat up, smiled, and patted the carpet next to him, mouthing, "Come over here." But there was too much between them—a huge expanse of rug, with a pattern that looked to Medio like swimming snakes, Kama's violent rocking in the chair, the coffee table, rising up huge to trip him as he walked.

"We're cramming Portuguese," Leslie said, pointing to a stack of tapes and workbooks on a nearby shelf. She looked at Chris and Medio. "You all are the future uncles, so you better learn, too. We're planning to be a bilingual household. I can already say, 'Yes, this is my daughter,' and 'Can you talk a bit more slowly, please?' "

Medio felt his face flame. His whole body tightened, except for his voice, which tumbled out of his mouth and into the room. "Have you also learned to say, 'This child belongs to someone else?' Or how about 'I bought my baby from a poor Latina who couldn't take care of the kids she already had?' " He was yelling now, rivers of words, his skin pulsing with rage. "Do you know the Portuguese for 'I can do anything I want because

I am a rich white American girl and my money runs the world'?"

Then he pushed past Leslie, yanked open the apartment door, and ran downstairs. He gripped the porch railing to make the world stand still. A carload of teenagers cruised the street, windows down. "Hey, look at the hair. It's the metal guy. It's Mr. Silver," one of them yelled. "What happened—somebody forget to polish you and you turned brown?" The car sped off in a cloud of laughter and exhaust.

Six nights a week, Medio Cabrales de Sanchez sprayed himself silver and carried his boom box to the Miami marina. He held his head still and flexed his legs wildly. He stood with his torso frozen and danced with his arms. The audience applauded, the sound filling his ears. While they clapped, he examined every small face in the crowd, searching for a wide upper lip, broad cheeks, eyes like his own. If she were here, would they recognize each other? Would Bruce and Sally put cautious hands on her shoulders and lead her away for ice cream?

"Are you married, Mr. Silver?"

"What's your real name?"

"If you touched something hot, would you melt?"

At home, he dumped his tips on the bathroom floor, then turned on the shower as hot as he could stand it. Flecks of silver fell from his hair, from his face, sluiced off his chest and back in eddies of mercury, dissolving to flat gray water, spiraling down the drain.

"Dear Mami," he wrote later. "The man I cook for is trying to get me a job at the best Miami restaurant. I live in the guest house on his property. But bad news—my girlfriend, Angela, has decided to transfer to a university in New York. So we will not be getting married. I'll send more money as soon as I have some." He would keep lying until he could finally tell her the truth, until he could write the letter that would shine like a newly minted coin: "Dear Mami, it is true the streets are golden. I have found her."

Nesting

Tara's mother made two cakes. The batter slipped in sheets into matching springform pans. Their lemon-poppyseed smell moistened the kitchen walls.

After an hour, she pulled them out. One had risen into a golden freckled belly. The other had folded in on itself, withdrawn from the sides of the pan. Its center was creased and pitted and somehow horrifying, like a face after a disfiguring accident. When she saw it, Tara's mother took in a sharp breath and sat down on a kitchen chair, her hand to her mouth.

"Mama, are you all right?" Tara said. "Is the cake broken?"

"Yes, I'm okay. We'll save the good cake. I don't know what happened." Then she lifted Tara into her lap and rocked her. "Something else, sweetie—we're going to have a baby."

From the living room, there was a creak as Tara's father rolled over on the couch.

In the taxi that came home from Sisters of Mercy Hospital were two potted plants with glossy leaves, and Tara's baby brother. The plants that came later were different, delivered to the house by fresh-faced young men. Circles of cut carnations, bloodless tea roses, baby's breath wound into wreaths. You were not supposed to water them. They were not meant to live.

At night, when the baby cried, Tara got a bottle from the refrigerator, held it under the hot-water faucet, then climbed into the crib and fed it to him. Sometimes she fell asleep and woke in the morning with her feet poking through the slats and her baby brother clinging to her chest like a barnacle. Then she climbed over the rail, got dressed, and went to second grade.

One day, Tara stayed late at school, scanning the spines of all the books on the sixth-grade shelf. When she came home, her father was at the kitchen table. Two empty beer cans sat on a stack of newspapers.

"I named him," Tara said. "Poe Corrin Sutter." Her mother's name was Corinne.

"Whatever you say, baby." Her father clutched his beefy hands together as if to prevent them from doing damage.

Tara couldn't wait for Poe to talk. She coaxed him, reading out loud from her homework, reports on Booker T. Washington and the story of Athena, sprung fully grown from her father's head.

It wasn't only that she craved conversation. It was this: Two Sutters had gone to the hospital, one tucked inside the other like those pear-bellied Russian nesting dolls her mother used to

have, and only one came back. Tara sat by the crib with a book
on her lap, willing Poe to remember, waiting for him to utter a
detail she could hold—the tickle of Corinne's hands on his
newborn head, the musky smell of her blood, the thin sweetness
of their mother's milk.

They played. The room was a spaceship, Poe the earthling
abducted to bring knowledge of tuna fish and yo-yos to far-flung
galaxies. Or it was an explorers' ship and Tara was captain, sailing
the globe for cinnamon and purple silks. She was fifteen and he
was eight. Their father slept on the pull-out couch. No one used
the master bedroom.

At night, when they couldn't sleep, Tara and Poe whispered
games into the dark channel between their beds.

"What's the most beautiful word in the English language?"
one of them would ask.

"Pellucid."

"Cellophane."

"Mellifluous."

"Corduroy."

"Umber."

They loved watery words, words soft as clouds sliding over the
moist face of the moon, thick-waisted words, smooth as avocado.
They liked words that filled their heads with liquid and blocked
the other sounds—the bottom cabinet squeaking open, the
empty glass smacking the tabletop, the television's sputter after
the programs stopped.

Poe talked. He talked to cashiers at the supermarket and to nuns
he met on the street, to police officers and gas-station attendants.

He read all of Tara's books, then began bringing home his own—Brecht and Little Ricky comic books, encyclopedias, romances. His appetites were endless and ecumenical. Once, he dragged her to an Indian sweat-lodge ceremony, another time to a Quaker meeting. By the time he was thirteen, he could recite the entire succession of the Hapsburg Empire and tell a joke about the Pope in three languages.

Between Poe's bursts of enthusiasm—for fractals one week, organic vegetables the next—he lapsed into silences that were gelid and complete. He would slip in from school and spend hours in their bedroom with the lights off. He emerged near midnight, pale, with rings under his eyes that looked like bruises. But he could not explain, not even to Tara, what demons pummeled him in the darkness.

When he talked, though, it was pure entertainment—a fair trade for the hours it took Tara to keep them fed, clothed, and reasonably organized. He followed her around the house, telling stories and imparting trivia, while she dusted and ironed, clipped rhododendrons, scrubbed the oven.

"Hey, look at those stacked lennies," he said once as she stretched to pinch clothespins to the underwear on the line.

It sounded to Tara like a kind of Norwegian pancake, or something tenth-grade boys would say in the locker room about the typing teacher's chest. Lennies, Poe explained, were lenticular clouds, the ones that looked like shredded laundry. His face was expectant and delighted when he told her this, like a person bestowing a gift. Outdoors, his eyes were the blue of swimming pools, just like Corinne's.

Poe's quiet times were Tara's worst days. She felt as though he had stumbled into a fissure in the earth. Once, she woke up at four in the morning to pee, and Poe turned over in his bed. "Don't go," he mumbled. When she returned from the bathroom, his knees were drawn up into a tense knot, and his head seemed to vanish in the top of his pajamas.

Over the years, Tara's father slowly got rid of everything that had belonged to Corinne. Clothes to Goodwill, letters into the fireplace. Tara found the set of Matrushka nesting dolls, nine in all, in a box under the bed. She uncapped the largest one, then the next, and the next, until they were lined up, identical and smiling, on her windowsill. The box said they were supposed to represent the march of generations.

Tara stared at them for hours, when she should have been studying. Sometimes she felt pity—not for the smallest doll, nestled inside, but for the big one, her hands clasped over that belly packed with eight other lives.

The silences between Poe's chatter grew longer. Once, he did not speak for nearly a month. At dinner, their father stared, as if his children were packages delivered to the wrong address. Eventually, he stopped joining them for meals—just came home, grabbed a bottle, and headed to the garage. Tara had no idea what he did all day, and she did not question the fifty dollars he handed her for groceries each week.

Tara was twenty-four and Poe was seventeen. She worked at an advertising agency all day and took graduate classes in computer science two evenings a week. Her apartment was a railroad flat, three rooms all in a row, and she called home every Saturday. Sometimes, Poe answered but wouldn't speak, and Tara held the receiver for one minute, two, three, just listening to him breathe.

One week, he didn't answer at all. Tara took the next train home.

"Your brother moved out," her father said. "Went to live with some fairy in Lancaster Village."

When Tara rang the bell, a man in sweats and bright green high-tops answered. "Hey, Poe, this must be that sister you've told me all about." Then he stuck out his hand. "I'm Steven."

The three spent the afternoon making tortillas from scratch, drinking tequila, listening to Ella Fitzgerald albums. There were tiger lilies in a coffee can on the table, magazines strewn everywhere. When Tara went to the bathroom, she couldn't help peeking into the medicine cabinet. Toothpaste, two boxes of condoms, and a pharmacy of little vials, all with Steven's name typed neatly on the labels. She didn't know whether to be panicked or relieved.

For a while, Poe sent postcards and called every few weeks. He'd quit high school. He got a job making salads in a restaurant. He and Steven were going to Baja in February.

"What's the most beautiful word, Tar?" he scribbled across the bottom of his postcards. And she wrote back: "Ethereal. Pudding. Undulate."

In April, the cards and phone calls suddenly stopped. The number was disconnected. The post office had no forwarding address. Tara's postcards came back, her own handwriting haunting her mailbox. "Sassafras. Phantom. Lull."

The Matrushka dolls stood in a line on Tara's desk. When she was having trouble with a computer program, she played with them. The dolls' faces were smooth as almonds, flat-featured. Did the largest one remember being young and small, she wondered, or was it the opposite—that the smallest was the oldest and had shrunk with age, shedding its earlier, ungainly selves?

On sticky nights when Tara couldn't sleep, she watched the dolls' silhouettes, the regular shadow steps of their heads. Once, her cat knocked a doll down at night. When Tara woke and saw the empty space between dolls number four and six, she stopped breathing for a second, until she saw the missing one, in two pieces, rolling gently on the floor.

It was September when the phone rang. Poe sounded frayed. There were sirens, traffic in the background.

"Tara, come get me. I'm scared."

"Okay, hang on. Just tell me where you are."

She hunched over the wheel, straining ahead. Poe stood on the southeast corner of Twelfth and Broadway. His clothes were dun-colored, his shoes cracked at the heels. His hair stuck out from under a faded Orioles cap. His arms stirred and pumped the air; his feet shuffled as if he were trying to dance in a shoe box. People walked around him in a wide ellipse.

She opened the door and her brother tumbled into the passenger seat. They were silent while Tara maneuvered through afternoon traffic. "Hey, Poe, what's the most beautiful word in the English language?" she said at a red light.

"Hospital," he said. "Hospital, hospital, hospital."

Such places always lay outside of town, beyond the beltway of Burger Kings, Christian bookstores, minimarts with signs— WE SELL NIGHT CRAWLERS—in the smeared windows. Then—a sudden stone wall, a too-green lawn, a building with porticos and, if you squinted from the road, bars on each rectangular window.

Tara started bringing the Matrushka dolls when she visited each week. Poe's doctor approved because they had no sharp edges. They played silently, taking the dolls apart, putting them back together. She combed Poe's hair, sewed buttons back on his shirts. She took away the cracked shoes and brought him a pair of bright green high-tops.

Poe's eyes filled up when she handed them over.

"Were you there when he died?" Tara asked.

Poe shook his head no, then nodded yes. Already his face had narrowed, the flesh drawing in near the bone. His cough was deep and rattled his whole body. "Sort of. His family didn't know. He let them think it was from a transfusion. We had a good friend, an intern in the hospital, who gave me scrubs. I'd pretend like I was a nurse's assistant. I sat there holding his hand. His folks wouldn't touch him."

Then his mouth crumpled. "How come, Tara?" Poe swept his arm through the whole line of dolls, and they clattered to the floor like bowling pins. Tara crawled on her knees, grabbing for the pieces as they rolled away.

Eight Matrushka dolls stood in a circle on Poe's nightstand, facing in. Tara imagined them having a meeting, reaching easy consensus. "We will grow," they whispered to one another. All eight smiled in unison.

Not always, Tara wanted to say. One rises and one falls. One lives and one shrinks to an hourglass of bone. One wears a plastic bracelet; the other takes her car keys and drives through the stone gates, into a sky splendid with stacked lennies. Always, she steered with her left hand and clutched the smallest doll in her right, holding and stroking it until finally the paint rubbed off and it was just a nugget, a mere suggestion, a small brown seed.

HEART

Liability

There is a weird and scary place of fusion, in certain West Coast towns, between old hippies and new survivalists. You wouldn't think so at first. You wouldn't think there'd be anything in common whatsoever between guys with long gray ponytails and teenaged daughters named Mango Starr and guys with lifetime memberships in the NRA and three months' supply of canned fruit in the basement.

I didn't think so, either, when I was twenty-three and ran away to Oregon. I thought all hippies were pacifists and all survivalists were rednecks and all people had the hots either for boys or for girls but not both. That's before the lines began to blur and I was proved wrong on all three counts.

I wasn't technically a runaway. What I mean by that is, I was over eighteen, I drove my own car out here from Baltimore, and nobody missed me much. My parents were too preoccupied with their own decomposing marriage, and my older sister, Constance, was busy climbing the corporate ladder straight out of denial and into the kind of oblivion only money can buy. My folks threw me a half-hearted good-bye party and Connie asked a few questions about what I planned to do way the hell out in California, and that was it. I didn't even bother to correct her and say it was Oregon, not California, I was headed for. I had the feeling that once I'd hit the beltway, they'd be back to their couples counseling and mutual funds, respectively.

I cut a zigzag path across the country, staying at youth hostels and with some old high school and college friends, and slept with practically everyone I met. Okay, that's a bit of an exaggeration. But this was before I worried much about AIDS—I mean, I knew it was happening, but I filed it away in the Remote Danger category, along with global warming and the threat of terrorism on American soil. That summer, sex seemed a fine way to seal an old friendship or embark on a new one. Got to where it was as casual as clinking beer mugs in some tavern fifteen miles off Route 80, and most encounters lasted as long as the head on a glass of Miller Lite.

Jimmy was the first. He and I had made out in sleeping bags one summer a long time ago at Camp Tok-a-Wisson. He hadn't changed much: same shaggy blond hair, same easy lope down the street. We went to the science museum; it made him happy to explain things about centrifugal force and the laws of thermodynamics. I was interested in the computer that took a picture of you and then showed how you'd look when you were seventy-five. I looked sort of like a cross between Margaret Thatcher and Betty Crocker, and Jimmy was sweet enough to say it was a new program and they didn't really have all the bugs out of the system.

We drank beer in some basement pub on University Avenue, and it was easy, once we were back at his apartment, to move from mushroom pizza and old camp stories to looking at photo albums on the couch, to my hands sliding the elastic off his pony-tail and his tongue taking a quiet inventory of my mouth. In the morning, we grinned over our juice and then I asked him which highway led to Chicago. He looked relieved, as if he'd been half-afraid I might get cozy after one night and start unloading Tampax in his perfectly tidy bathroom. Not to worry: I had no intention of staying long enough to leave a shadow on the sheets.

Next, I visited Charlotte, my freshman-year roommate. Except she wasn't Charlotte anymore; she was calling herself Chazz and had about five earrings in each ear and twenty kinds of herbal tea in her cabinets. I checked out the bookshelf and the video collection just to confirm my guess: yep, the hot-pink *Lesbian Sex* book right next to *Rubyfruit Jungle,* not to mention her own copy of *Lianna,* the box a little wilted from use. We baked cranberry muffins so she could eat the crown and I could eat the bottom, just like we did all through college, and she made me a cup of Roastaroma because it was the closest thing to coffee.

Then she put her hand on my knee and said she'd always thought I was beautiful. "You did?" I said, and next thing I knew, we were rolling on her futon, hands inside each other's clothes. I licked my way around the crescent of her ear, each tiny silver stud a milepost. What surprised me was how I knew where to touch her, even though I'd never done that with a woman before, and how, when I did, I felt my own body rise and open.

But in the morning, Chazz wanted me to meditate with her in front of a little statue of a goddess with too many arms. Then she wondered out loud whether she should tell the woman she was seeing about our fling, even though they were officially non-monogamous. I began to feel like my clothes were wrapped too tight. "Whoops," I said, unfolding my map on her kitchen table. "I was meaning to get to Kansas City before dark."

By the time I reached Portland two weeks later, I was calling myself bisexual. I knew there were folks on both sides of the fence who had a problem with that—felt it was greedy, or otherwise a sort of cheating, moral flip-floppiness about something that ought to be a matter of principle and pride. I just didn't get why a person should have to choose, except in each instance as it came along. I mean, I like pinball and art-house flicks with subtitles. Men's Jockey briefs and silk blouses that fall over my skin like moonlight. Courvoisier and Ho Hos.

I didn't know Portland from Poughkeepsie, but I had the phone number of a friend of a friend from college who said they always needed new counselors at the battered women's shelter, and the West appealed to me as a place beyond the adhesive grasp of guilt and expectation. I was twenty-three and already felt exhausted by history, tired of living in a city where the buildings wore two hundred years of grime and you could trace corruption back three generations in some families, like a kink in the DNA. Politics was a pretty curdled enterprise when I became a sentient being; I remember getting my mouth scrubbed out with green janitor's soap for yelling, "Richard Nixon is a fucking liar" from the top of the jungle gym. I was twelve and barely knew what Nixon had done wrong, but it was something my uncle Max had screamed at the TV.

A few years after that, my parents' arguments changed from occasional eruptions to a constant grinding friction, and I realized I could become the daughter of a divorced daughter of a divorced daughter. I was dead set not to get tangled in anything a lawyer would have to get me out of.

After college, I saved money by living at home while I ran the lights for a small theater company. I worked nights, so my hours off frequently coincided with the onset of my mother's migraines—which began moments after my father said something like "I thought all that goddamn therapy was supposed to make our marriage more *fun*," then splashed his coffee into the sink. I'd pat my mom on the shoulder, hand her the Kleenex and the ice pack, nudge her in the direction of her darkened study. I was so good at the routine, I could do it in my sleep.

But nothing changed. Connie voted for Reagan—not once, which could have been a temporary brain lapse, but *twice*—my parents fired their therapist and found a new one, and the city pulled the plug, literally, on the theater company's funding. We were in the middle of a run and had to light a show by giving flashlights to the audience and cuing them where to point, because we couldn't afford the electric bill. I figured it was my cue to exit, stage left. To head west, before I got sucked into everyone else's despair. While there was still time to do something different.

When I first got to Portland, I drove back and forth across the bridges, north and south on the numbered avenues, just trying to get a picture of the place. Actually, I was looking for the ghetto—not because I wanted to live in some blasted-out row house with used needles in the alleyway, but because the next neighborhood over might be cheap and undiscovered and reasonably safe. That jittery line between the crackheads and the Yuppies.

It was a muzzy pink dusk, and I drove around, hunting for a corner where men in sleeveless undershirts would be sitting in lawn chairs, watching boxing on a black-and-white TV with the cord snaked through somebody's screen door. Or their teenaged

daughters, all arms and lips, braiding each other's hair and hoot-
ing at boys from the safety of a second-floor window. I cruised
with the windows down, my ears and eyes tuned for a boom box
pumping calypso or salsa, and old ladies with clasp purses cluck-
ing tongues as they walked by.

I circled, looking for the city's messy, noisy heart. But I couldn't
find it.

All around me, cars grumbled into driveways, people emerged
with grocery bags and car seats, doors opened and closed, dinner
smells—curry in one house, pot roast in another—leaked out
onto the street. I passed a bungalow where a man with a mus-
tache was out front, clipping dahlias with a pair of sewing shears.
Then another man opened the door, called, "Tony, soup's on—"
and smiled when he saw the bouquet. Their house smelled like
roasted garlic and sourdough.

Next door, a teenager with a ponytail met the pizza delivery
guy at the door. "Okay, that's one vegetarian, one pineapple and
Canadian bacon—don't even ask; it's for my brother, the human
garbage disposal—and—hey, Mom, I need a check to pay for all
this." The pizza guy pocketed the check and loped down to his
car, a dirty white hatchback with a little Domino's flag breezing
from the antenna.

Downtown, I saw a guy in a kelly green vest strut around with
a broom and a long-handled dustpan, sweeping up McDonald's
wrappers from the brick sidewalks. In Baltimore, people who
walked around the streets with cleaning implements were either
wacko or sentenced to community service, but this guy looked
happy and normal, as if he might actually get paid to pluck up
trash from the street.

Every drinking fountain I saw was broken; they kept bubbling water all the time, and there was no button to push. People just bent down and slurped. Near the river, on the downtown side, were a bunch of pink condos that looked like accessories for a train set. And a wide stretch of lawn striped gold and green in the setting sun, so vivid that it hurt my eyes. Just when it was all starting to make me feel a little creepy, like I'd stepped into some tabletop rendition of a model city, I spotted a billboard for a special savings account at Far West Federal Bank. There were pictures of a diamond ring, a fur coat, a tropical island, and the words FOR THE LITTLE THINGS YOU WANT IN LIFE. Underneath, in loopy red spray paint, someone had written, "Yeah. Like socialism."

I drove toward the billboard, past a twenty-four-hour bowling alley, a head shop with a huge mural of an eye, and a Winchell's Donuts with a police cruiser out front, and parked the car on a corner that reeked of patchouli. A couple of teenagers leaned against the window of a video store; I hadn't seen so much tie-dye since I watched Woodstock on video. But not just tie-dye— long hair on the boys, long underwear and hiking boots on the girls, and all of them with these dumb, stoned, happy expressions. Hadn't anybody told these kids it was over, that all the flowers had gone to soldiers and John Lennon was dead? Hadn't the bad news made it over the mountains?

I followed a girl in a gauzy skirt into some throwback veggie café where everything, even the desserts, seemed to be made of ground-up chickpeas. Then I looked on the bulletin board for shared housing. I had too many condoms in my backpack to pass the screening at any place calling for "Peaceful lesbian to join vegan nonsmoking household with 3 wimmin and 2 cats named Vita and Virginia." Besides, I liked the occasional hamburger, on a hard-crowned sourdough roll, with barbecue chips on the side.

I skipped the cards with *women* spelled wrong and scribbled down the number for one signed "Ernesto." The handwriting was small and square, like architects' notes on blueprints, and I appreciated his brevity: "Spare room, need someone to fill it. Nice old wood house, no shag carpet or poodles, plenty hot water, $210 plus utils." I imagined Ernesto as an East Coast migrant like myself, a guy who subscribed to *Harper's* but sneered at Wall Street, a thirtyish wanderer in Levi's and horn-rims.

Instead, Ernesto—"Name's really Ernest, but everyone calls me Esto," he said immediately—turned out to be closer to my father's age, with skin so leathery, it looked like he took it off and baked it each night before zipping it back on. He had droopy St. Bernard eyes and, if I'd peered closely, the jaundice of incipient liver damage in the whites. But I wasn't looking. Didn't want to see—or be seen—at that close range. Esto took me on a tour of the house, proudly pointing out the claw-foot tub he'd rescued from the dump, but I was mostly interested in a room with a good snug door, so I could carry on my sex life in the style to which my road trip had accustomed me.

Esto introduced me to the other housemates: Lilly, a former philosophy major who painted houses for a living; Johan, a cheerful Austrian émigré who taught phys ed at the local high school; and Esto's sixteen-year-old daughter, Cloud, who stared at me through a thick scrim of red hair and said only, "I have dibs on the bathroom after ten P.M."

Everyone seemed strange but benign, which was exactly what I'd hoped and expected from the Northwest. Esto told me there were no house meetings, just a casual dinner once a week, and few rules. "It's a drug-free household," he said almost apologetically, and I was about to ask, like a smart-ass, if that included

Snickers bars and black tea, but then I saw the pack of Marlboro stiffening his shirt pocket and smelled a whiff of beer, so decided I'd better keep quiet.

"Basically, we're a 'live and let live' kind of crowd," he said. That suited me fine. I was tired of scraping linguine off dinner dishes my parents had abandoned in the middle of an argument, sick of being the only one of the four of us—my stockbroker sister included—who remembered to buy vitamin C or take the dog for a walk or show up at the neighborhood meeting to discuss the crack vials littering the playground. I was tired of staying up nights picking my cuticles till they bled and wondering if Connie was ever going to fall in love or develop an ethical soul, or whether my parents were going to chip away at each other's happiness until they died, or divorce while they were still young enough to start over.

"Sounds great," I told Esto. I felt perfectly content to settle in without phone calls and questions, family names and resumes, without having to feel bad about other people's messed-up lives. Esto didn't ask for references, and he wanted the rent in cash because he was trying to secede from the capitalist economy. If you were serious about that, I thought, you'd let me barter rent for some heavy-duty cleaning—which I noticed the place could use—but I just drove to the bank and came back with my first month's installment in soft fifty-dollar bills.

He folded the money into his shirt pocket without counting it or even glancing at the bills, as if it pained him to traffick in something so crass as a financial exchange. Then he sandwiched my hand in both of his and said, "I'm glad your path carried you here." Normally, that was the sort of line that made me want to retch, but Esto was so solemn and earnest about it, his eyes practically soupy with tears, that I just met his gaze, held on, and said, "Well, thanks. Me, too."

At the battered women's shelter, I could tell the staff was testing me. On the first day, during check-ins at the meeting, the head case manager introduced herself by saying, "Hi, I'm Sue, and I'm a radical lesbian separatist. If you last any longer than our previous intern, you can ask me what that means." Another case manager, who wore a tiny knitted pouch on a dirty string around her neck, described herself as a "fat hippie pagan dyke," and somebody else said she'd been a Buddhist monk for eleven years. I guessed I'd sleep with one of them by New Year's, but I wasn't sure which. That was the great thing about living in Portland, the tolerance for uncertainty. I could do what I wanted, even if I didn't know what that was exactly.

The staff all talked about the hot line and the shelter and how we weren't supposed to rescue the women, but empower them to save themselves. "Are you a crisis junkie?" Sue asked, and I made them all laugh by saying I used to be but that now I was in withdrawal, going to CJA—Crisis Junkie Anonymous—meetings and using chocolate as a sort of methadone. They smiled, but they didn't realize how true it was—not the meetings, but the secession. I was the last person who was likely to try yanking someone else out of her emotional muck. I knew all it left you with was tired arms and that slack, dead-end feeling when the adrenaline of emergency subsided.

At home, things were pretty much the way Esto had described. House dinners were a little strange, almost as if the five of us had met by default at one of those restaurants where you pay good money to sit with people you don't know. Johan always ate two helpings and chirped praise for whoever had cooked, even the night Cloud served us microwaved burritos that were still frosty in the middle. Lilly talked endlessly about the houses she worked on, how unhealthy the owners were, with their synthetic carpets and particleboard shelves and freezers full of hormone-injected beef. I wanted to say, If you're painting the house, why are you looking in their freezers? but it seemed to violate some citywide pact of nonaggression.

I'd been in town only a month, but it seemed Portland suffered a case of terminal niceness. Maybe it was something in those water fountains—which, it turned out, weren't broken, but just bubbled all the time, according to the wishes of the eccentric guy who had them built something like a hundred years ago. When I took the bus home from work, people queued up the way they do at theme parks, gathering obediently at the symbol-coded bus shelters for different regions of the city—purple raindrop to the airport, orange deer into the West Hills, brown beaver toward Southeast and Reed College. No one ever lurched down the aisle with a tin cup in one hand and a ripped Bible in the other, proclaiming the end of the world, which happened about every other day in Baltimore. I didn't have to signal for my stop by yelling, "Hey, HEY, let me out!" because the signal bar actually worked, and when I stepped down, the driver said, "Bye, miss, thanks for riding," and smiled like he meant it.

At Fred Meyer, a store where you could buy canned peas and tire chains and maxipads all under one roof, a worker came up to me, looking truly concerned, and said. "Are you finding everything you need?" Once I dashed out of the library, frantic about getting a parking ticket, only to find that some Samaritan had fed two more quarters into my meter.

Even the weather unnerved me; spring wasn't a change of season, but a kind of seepage. In Baltimore, we had thunderstorms, serrated flashes of lightning, thumps across the horizon. Like the gods had lost their cool and just started heaving furniture at one another. When they were done, though, the air glistened, astringent. The storms actually swept some debris out of the way. In Portland, the weather never reached that pitch; it was one long postnasal drip of rain, skies like an old hankie. Every now and then a thin finger of sun would come out and scrape the pavement once, then vanish into a fist of gray.

It was all a bit weird. I was used to shrill voices, jangly disharmonies, defensive postures. It's how I knew, as a five-year-old terrified of the dark and abandonment, that my parents were still at home, snarling each other into misery. Connie and I fought all the time; it was how you got to know people. Here, I couldn't seem to find a grip: Johan hummed through his days like a windup toy, and Lilly was insubstantial as chiffon. Cloud lived in the house as if she were burglarizing it, slipping in and out of rooms, all ghostly foundation makeup and ripped fishnets and irritated glares.

Esto, at least, was interesting, with his weary face and his way of peering directly into your eyes, as if he could see the thing you were about to say but didn't. One morning I found him crumpled over the comics, dabbing tears with a breakfast napkin. "It's so sad," he said, pointing to that day's installment of "Blondie." "They're always arguing. They don't realize how good they have it."

"Read 'Peanuts,' " I said. "Snoopy is very wise," and I patted him on the shoulder. Cloud grabbed a piece of toast and shrugged into her coat. "You two are really pathetic."

Esto was no Ozzie Nelson, but he tried to pay attention to Cloud. Every time he reached out, she ducked. If he made a mushroom omelette on a Sunday morning, Cloud claimed she'd become a vegan and didn't eat eggs. If he mentioned a Sweet Honey in the Rock concert, she rolled her eyes. If he asked her what happened at school, she muttered, "The usual brainwashing." She rarely left her room except to go to school and to soak in the tub late at night, her boom box on loud, Janis Joplin's voice clawing its way through the lavender steam.

My room was next to the bathroom. When I heard water start to gurgle into the tub, I'd tap on the bathroom door to ask Cloud if I could come in and brush my teeth while her bath filled. It got to be a kind of ritual: we shared a spool of cinnamon dental floss and had brief conversations punctuated by the *plik-plik* of floss against our teeth.

"Homework?" I asked once, pointing at a thick book she'd left on the toilet seat, its pages wavy from water.

"World War Two," Cloud nodded.

"Oh. Have you read—"

"Anne Frank? When I was twelve. My teacher told us we should keep journals because someday people might be reading them. And I was like, *hello,* but Anne Frank had to die in a concentration camp before anyone cared what she had to say." Cloud hit the play button on her boom box and tugged her hair into a rough ponytail.

"G'night, Linden."

"Good night."

The walls were thin, and Cloud's midnight soaks became a sort of lullaby—the gentle sploshing of water, Janis's ragged yowls. At least someone was trying to pierce the surface. I held on to that raspy yearning and followed it into sleep.

I called Baltimore once a week—first my sister, then my parents—and talked to each person for ten minutes. Connie was working fourteen-hour days and eating Chinese takeout in her BMW. When she started to lecture me about coming back to the real world and opening an IRA, I clicked lightly on the disconnect button and pretended we had call waiting. My parents were still seeing the gestalt therapist and were considering a weeklong intimacy retreat; I didn't want to know the details.

"And you?" they sometimes remembered to ask.

"Fine," I said, raising a fence around the word with my voice. No one asked any more questions.

Which was just as well. Because I slept with people as if the Pope might get elected president and outlaw sex. I slept with people like I had a terminal illness and needed regular orgasms to keep me this side of death's door. Boys, girls, my colleague the fat hippie pagan dyke and my colleague the former monk and Michaelangelo, the psychedelic-drug user turned born-again pharmacist who lived up the street.

I loved how the world fell away during sex. At first, my mind would spit images like a wire service: the antiabortion picketers screaming "Murderer" outside the clinic; the little kid next door with the plummy bruise on her cheek. The fact that I hadn't seen Cloud in four days. Then gradually, the hands on my body kneaded me into senselessness. I forgot how old I was, the name of my first puppy, and how much money my mom would need to live if my folks ever split up. I hungered for that moment of blind sensation: *There,* I thought each time, I want to live *there,* on that pulsing island south of my heart.

I discovered how little sex had to do with gender; I wasn't interested in my lovers specifically, but in their capacity to move me past the chatter in my head, carry me away from myself. Sometimes I'd wake curled spoon-style against a warm back and long, slightly greasy hair, or an auburn buzz cut and double-pierced ears, and I'd have to peek under the sheets to remember if I was with a guy or a girl.

But there was one night I do remember, one of the few when I slept alone. I woke to a room full of orange light, and a smell that, for one surreal second, made me hungry for s'mores. I pushed aside my curtain and screamed. Esto's old Buick—parked on cinder blocks just feet from the wooden porch—was lapped in flames. I yanked a T-shirt over my head and ran down the hall, pounding on everyone's doors: *Hey, fire. Get up. Esto's car—I'm calling nine one one.*

In minutes, the truck was there—nine men with hip boots and axes hacking at the garage and soaking Esto's car with hoses. "Any idea how the incident started?" one asked. We shrugged. Johan immediately became Mr. Congeniality, chatting up the firefighters about what kind of push-ups they did. Cloud lurked in the corner of the kitchen, wearing a stained silk kimono and black lipstick. She wouldn't look at Esto. Lilly buzzed around making nondairy hot chocolate with rice milk and carob powder. Later, after the fire truck crunched away, Esto said it was his fault—he'd tossed a cigarette butt out the window, thinking it was out, but obviously it wasn't, and he hoped he hadn't scared us to death.

"Shit," Cloud said, and marched back upstairs. But the rest of us tried to make him feel better, saying it could happen to anyone and luckily no one had been hurt and we were sure he'd be more careful in the future. When Esto's eyes got wet and red, Johan started sponging crumbs off the table, and Lilly offered more hot chocolate, but it was cold by then. Esto's tears splatted onto the wood. When I leaned over to give his shoulders a quick squeeze, I smelled something more potent than carob in his cup.

The scorched car sat there like some post-Armageddon arti-fact, and we all tried to get back to normal, such as normal was. But then, a few weeks later, I couldn't find the electric space heater that we usually kept in the bathroom. Cloud poked her head out of her bedroom when I knocked, and she said she hadn't seen it. Johan looked puzzled: "Heater? Never use it," and Lilly started to lecture me about how electric appliances were making our neurons misfire. Esto was still at work, but I tapped on his door reflexively. The wood was warm. A buzzing inside. I pushed it open: There was the heater, cranked up to high, with an old India-print bedspread bunched on the floor, way too close for my comfort.

When I picked it up, I saw papers fanned underneath. I bent down; on top was a price list from a gun show, and under it a newsletter headlined WHO CAN'T YOU TRUST? from a group called Defenders of the American Nation. In the corner next to the clothes hamper, I counted thirty-six cans of evaporated milk.

I could feel blood beating inside my ears, and a wave of nausea churned through me. I was snooping; I knew that, and I knew it was wrong, and I couldn't stop. On the dresser, where most peo-ple would keep their combs and spare change, there was a set of Tarot all laid out, with the devil card smack in the middle. And

126

above that, stuck into the frame of Esto's old streaked mirror, were three Polaroid photos.

The top one showed a brown-haired man in a blue-and-green Guatemalan tunic, both his arms circling a woman with wavy reddish hair, a spray of freckles, and a mouth still poised in the loose posture of a kiss. They both wore leis of wilted daisies. I almost didn't recognize Esto without the pleated pouches around his eyes, the loose jowl. In that inscrutable printing I remembered from the housing notice, he had written, "Our un-wedding—ha-ha—1968."

A yellow piece of paper stuck out from behind the picture. I unfolded it carefully: a whole page of typed vows, beginning, "Let our union be blessed not by church or state, but by sun and earth, stars and moon. I promise to support your choices until the end of this life, and beyond." It went on, a total hippie cliché, all about embracing each other without judgment or possession and allowing the winds of time to exert their power and blah, blah, blah. The last promise was "to use our love as a generative force for good in this fucked-up world."

I read that one about five times, and on the fifth read, some membrane inside me snapped and I started leaking tears onto the crinkled paper. I wasn't even sure why I was crying—because the world was still so fucked-up, or because it was heartbreaking that Esto and this woman had once thought they could do anything about it, or because she looked so pretty and buoyant and maybe I'd never even get to meet her. I was a mess, almost as bad as Esto with the comics. Next thing you knew, I'd be crying at commercials for long-distance phone service. I sniffled into my sleeve and tucked the wedding vows back behind the picture.

In the next photo, the woman was pregnant, her huge belly

draped in a calico-print peasant skirt, her breasts bare, a gleaming purple eggplant in each hand. "Celine with Cloud inside," read Esto's caption. The bottom photo looked more recent, a close-up of Cloud snapped maybe a year or two ago. She sat on a swing, her hands open in her lap. Red hair braided into two smooth skeins; no makeup; eyes angled down, as if she didn't want to meet the picture taker head-on. I pulled the picture out of the frame and turned it over. The same square print: "August '83. Celine gone. Now what?"

That's when I heard footsteps on the porch. Esto was home. My hands were starting to sweat, and the room's smell—like a frat party the morning after—was making me dizzy. I yanked the plug on the heater, slipped Cloud's picture into my back pocket, and hustled out of the room.

We elected Johan to talk to Esto about fire danger and electric bills, and Esto seemed sad afterward, slumping around like the gravitational tug was twice as strong on him as on everybody else. I didn't tell anybody about the canned milk or the other stuff. I figured it was Esto's business, and as long as he didn't burn down the house, I shouldn't pry. After all, I didn't want him cross-examining me about my lack of discrimination in sexual partners, or asking what those leather bracelet things were doing on my nightstand.

Things got stranger. One afternoon, I found Esto's cigarettes in the vegetable crisper drawer of the fridge and the salad greens in the bathtub. He said he thought it would save water if he washed them all at once. But he left the tap running and nearly ruined the hallway floor. Another night, he backed his car onto the front lawn, set the sprinkler on the roof, and watered the grass until it was a swamp. He disciplined the cat by closing it in the pantry, where, of course, it freaked out and peed all over the cornflakes. He said we should all stop reading the newspaper, because if we focused energy on what America was doing in Nicaragua, it would only get worse.

He dangled a crystal, the size of a horse's tooth, over his plate to decide whether he should eat something—if the crystal moved in a spiral, the answer was yes; if it swung like a pendulum, he turned the food down. And he smelled like a fucking distillery—not just on Saturday nights or rainy weekday afternoons but all the time. Still, I was crossing all sorts of behavioral boundaries myself, and it was hard to know the difference between eccentricity and danger.

One day, Esto and I had a huge argument about whether battered women were actually choosing that experience in order to further their cosmic growth, or something like that. It started because I was reading about how the cops in Philadelphia dropped a bomb on those MOVE people and burned up two blocks' worth of houses. I slapped the paper on the table and said, "They ought to impeach the mayor and elect Ramona Africa instead." I didn't really believe it—I thought the MOVE people sounded paranoid and mean—but I'd gotten in the habit of saying outrageous things at meals just to get a rise out of someone. And Esto bit.

"I don't know about that, Linden," he said, his whole face creased with concern. "Those MOVE people died because it was their time to move on."

"What about the kids? What about the neighbors who lost their houses? Was it *their* time to become homeless?" I could feel my pulse break into an excited trot, my skin itch with the ecstasy of argument. "Come on, Esto, you can't believe they woke up that morning and thought, Gee, I sure hope the cops bomb my block today."

"Well, not consciously. But people do create their own reality, you know. So maybe there was something they needed to learn about, um, vulnerability or violence, or—"

"Wait a second. Like women whose husbands slap them around? You're saying they *need* that experience? Jesus, Esto. That's insane!"

Then I heard myself, and I realized it was the same tone of voice my sister used with me when I told her that corporations were poisoning the earth and squashing the human spirit. So I stopped yelling, put my hand on his, and said, "Esto, I just don't think anybody would choose self-destruction if they really believed they had a choice." I left him sitting at the table, dangling his crystal over the baked potatoes.

I nearly collided with Cloud on my way out of the room.

"You don't know what the hell you're talking about," she hissed. "How do you know what people will choose? You don't have any idea." She had four cereal bowls stacked in her hands, and they clattered against one another.

"Hey, steady, Cloud. Watch those dishes."

"My mom killed herself." She bit each word.

"Oh, God, Cloud. I didn't—I had no idea. I'm really sorry."

"Yeah, well, she left a note saying her time on this earthly plane was up and she was ready to go on to the next world. Big help for the ones who had to go on living in this one." She shrugged, and the cereal bowls leaned dangerously to the left.

I thought about the gun-show flyers in Esto's room. "Cloud, how did she . . . What did she . . ."

"Total drama, just like her. Drove to the Gorge with a bottle of Nembutal and a Jack Daniel's chaser. Took the cops three days to find her. It was August. It was awful. He"—and she jerked her elbow toward the kitchen—"totally lost it. I had to go identify her. I saw the stupid yin-yang tattoo on her butt and told the morgue guy, 'Yeah, that's my mom all right.' Then I threw up in a wastebasket and a cop had to drive me home."

I reached out to hug her, but she ducked under the bridge of my arm. "Shit. Cloud, I don't know what to say." But it didn't matter, because she was already in the kitchen, dropping bowls one by one into the dirty sink.

At work, I kept busy answering the hot line, escorting women to the emergency room, and calling shelters all over the county to beg for bed space. I read about denial and intervention and family systems and the cycle of abuse, and about how silence just perpetuates the whole stinking mess. At home, though, the silence had its benefits. It was refreshing to emerge from the shower and drip down the hall, some skinny-hipped boy or butch girl following me in a towel, and know that Connie wasn't going to lecture me about morals or sexually transmitted diseases. Relieving to announce, over tofu meatballs and spaghetti one night, that I was thinking of getting my nose pierced, and the only question anyone asked was, "Which side?"

"The left," I said, and Esto smiled. "That's good. It's lucky, the left side. All the ancient priestesses had their noses pierced there."

Cloud snorted. "I am so done with the whole piercing thing. It's so . . . bourgeois."

"Like trying to speak high school French with a perfect

accent, *ma chérie?*" I said, and she actually smiled. So did Esto. Maybe he was crazy; maybe he knew things. I reached up and touched my left nostril, the small hillock where the stud would go. I could imagine the sting, thrilling and painful, as it went in.

Esto began to talk more and more oddly, in a way that reminded me a little of Noam Chomsky and a little of Billy Graham and scared me a lot. He believed the government was corrupt all the way from NATO to the local zoning board, that people who committed crimes just needed to find their inner light, and that we needed guns to protect ourselves against the "suits"—by whom he meant everyone from our mail carrier to Ronald Reagan. Johan and Lilly and I started eating faster, rinsing and stacking our plates while Esto was still going on about how the school system's plan to teach phonics to second graders was really a form of mind control.

Then there was the week he stopped going to work because, he said, the ventilation system was full of the stuff that gave people Legionnaires' disease. His room stank of dope and beer, and at night we all glanced at each other edgily, then slipped off to our own rooms. Once or twice, I knocked on Esto's door, ostensibly to say good night, but really to listen for the gargle of the electric heater. He kept swiping it from the bathroom, and I didn't trust anymore that he'd turn it off.

Cloud withdrew, too, stopped taking her midnight baths, let her hair mat into those unfortunate white-girl dreadlocks, and hoarded dishes in her room until, every few days, we had to ask her to bring the bowls and cups back downstairs. A few times, I found myself about to do something big sisterish, like pat her shoulder and say, "Parents really suck, don't they?" or see if she wanted to go to the Dairy Queen, but it seemed so inadequate and clichéd. A double scoop in a sugar cone wasn't going to fix Cloud's life.

Besides, I was preoccupied with my own. All that sex was making me sad—the same depleted feeling I had in those huge warehouse grocery stores. Surrounded by so much food, cheap and right there for the taking, it's easy to forget what hunger is. Or maybe sex had lost its power to silence my brain. Warm fingers traced my ear, and I'd be thinking about Esto and Cloud and Celine. About the vows I saw yellowing in Esto's room: "I promise to support your choices until the end of this life, and beyond." Is that what love meant—that you had to stand there waving a supportive good-bye while someone toppled off into the next plane, wherever the hell that was? Esto looked so goofy in their un-wedding picture, with that daisy necklace and his arms circling Celine as if he planned never, ever to let go. I'd think about that, and meanwhile a tongue would be lapping at the ticklish slope of my inner thigh, and all I wanted to do was weep.

My nights were starting to slur together, one long sticky chain of bodies, and while I remembered a gesture here, a voice there, I couldn't match them up to the people they belonged to. Someone said my feet smelled like the olive groves on Mykonos. Someone tugged on my hair when she came. Someone ate only fruit, nuts, and yogurt and had a serious problem with gas. Someone's tattoo was a maple leaf clenched like a fist. No one stayed long enough to drive me crazy by leaving the newspaper sections all skewed, instead of tucking them back in order. I wanted someone, at least, to ask me what I'd dreamed.

One afternoon, I got off the bus from work, rounded the corner, and saw two cop cars, their sirens off, their lights dancing red, white, and blue like the Republican National Convention. The cops had Esto on the porch, and he was naked, screaming, "Let me go, let me gooooo!" His voice scraped my spine, rasping over each vertebra. I had to look away from his scrawny brown limbs.

The cops trundled him off the porch, each one holding an arm or leg, and folded Esto into the back of one of the cruisers, then went in the house to get some of his clothes. "What happened?" they asked Johan, who, I gathered, had been the one to call, and he said he'd come home for lunch and found Esto lying on the living room floor, a near-empty jug of Chianti next to him. Esto wouldn't stop drinking, and then he took off all his clothes and wanted to go outside. When Johan tried to hold him back, he started kicking and flailing and grabbed a chef's knife off the drain board in the kitchen. That's when Johan called 911.

"We'll take him to detox," one cop said—a young one, with a face innocent as banana cream pie. "But after that, he'll be back, unless he signs himself into rehab. What's his last name?"

We all looked at the porch, as if Esto's name was going to be written there on the dirty hemp mat.

"I don't know," I said. Johan shrugged. Lilly twisted the fringe on her skirt.

"And his age?" More silence.

"He's an Aries," Lilly said. "But I guess that's pretty obvious."

The cop clapped his notebook shut. "And you people live together?" he said. "Fine, whatever. We'll go take your friend to dry out. You'll see him again in a couple days. Meanwhile, you might want to find out a little more about him."

We followed the cops onto the sidewalk and stood in a line in size order—Lilly, then Johan, then me—like kids in a *Dick and Jane* reader—to wave good-bye to Esto. He was conked out in the molded-plastic backseat. The spinning lights made my head hurt, and for a minute I felt horribly dizzy, as if I were falling into a place beyond noise, past protest, so far away that no hands could reach to grab anyone away from the edge.

I looked up, and there was Cloud leaning out her bedroom window, watching the whole thing through those flames of hair. The cops started their cars, turned on their sirens. We stood there because we did not know what else to do. "Ernest William Kindall!" Cloud yelled from the second floor, loud enough to break something. "Kindall! Kindall! Kindall!" As the cars pulled away, her voice nearly drowned in their widening, whining arcs of loss.

I moved out two days later. It was too weird to stay put, with Johan acting aggressively cheerful, as if his radiant good health could compensate for Esto's weakened state, and Lilly practically in mourning, dressing in black and baking endless no-sugar brownies and wheat-free cakes. She had this notion that everything wrong with Esto could be cured if he purified his diet, cut out all sugar, refined flour, preservatives, yeast, salt, and pretty much anything else that made food taste good. And Cloud? I assumed she was still alive, only because the dishes kept dwindling from the cupboards. None of us had the heart to ask her to bring them back downstairs.

The night Esto left was a Thursday, house dinner night, but no one offered to cook. I actually started to bake some potatoes, but caught myself as I was scrubbing the fifth one, suddenly remembering there were only four of us. I couldn't stand the thought of sitting across from Esto's empty chair or meeting the question in Cloud's eyes: How could this happen? I could bake a hundred potatoes, and it would never be enough.

Instead, I took a bath, wrapped myself in a towel, and ate a tuna sandwich in my room. Esto had given me an old wool poncho I was using as an area rug. It smelled like him: cigarettes, stale beer, cedar incense. I sat there and played with the fringe, braiding and unbraiding it. And then, through my open window, the explosive shatter of glass. Once. Twice. Jangling against the driveway. I tossed the poncho over my head and ran downstairs.

I could see her through the curtain at the back door. Cloud stood in the driveway, liquor bottles clustered at her feet like bowling pins. She grabbed one, twisted off the cap, chugged once, then flung it overhand onto the asphalt. Again. Again, wiping her mouth roughly, letting liquor drip onto her shirt.

"Cloud?" I opened the door, started to walk toward her.

"Mom?" Her voice like a nail being wrenched from a board, an arc of surprise, resistance, pain.

"What? No, Cloud, it's me, Linden."

She blinked. "I knew that. Go away."

"Cloud, what are you doing?"

She teetered a little. Her legs were bare under a satin miniskirt, her feet in a pair of ridiculous spike-heeled sandals. "What does it look like I'm doing? Getting rid of some shit." And she sucked from a bottle of scotch, raising it to her face in a wild swoop, then dropping her elbow to smash the bottle at her feet.

"Cloud, don't. Stop. I mean it."

"Why?"

What could I tell her? Because it's bad for the flowers. Because you'll cut your feet. Because tomorrow your dad will come home from detox and stop at the minimart for a bottle of wine on the way. Because there's always another fight, another migraine, and you're just a kid.

I held out my arms. "Because it's late. Come on. Come inside."

Cloud grabbed the bourbon, raised it overhead, then brought it down. But there was no muscle in it, just a collapse of wrist, a loosening of fingers as she let the bottle go. She picked her way through the galaxy of broken glass, stumbled up the back steps, came close enough that I could smell the liquor on her mouth, dark and harsh.

"I'll clean it up tomorrow," she said. "And Linden?"

"Yeah?"

"When you leave, you can't take my mom's poncho." Then she let the back door slam behind her. I held myself under the stiff wool and watched the stain of alcohol inch toward the street.

Nobody helped me move. I carried my Salvation Army desk and the cartons I'd been using as bookshelves up three flights of stairs to a studio apartment that smelled of cat piss. On such short notice, I couldn't afford to be picky. The landlady said the previous tenant had skipped out, leaving her futon and about a year's supply of brewer's yeast and a note that said she and her "feline spirit soul mates" were joining the Rainbow Gathering. I'd never heard of that, but Kalia, the one at work with the little knitted pouch, told me it was this traveling hippie carnival that drifts around the United States all summer, proclaiming peace and love for the environment and leaving huge rings of smashed-down grass in the places where they've pitched their tents and parked their painted VW buses. Kalia used to be into it, but now she thought it was full of really negative energy.

"Oh," I said.

I'd never set up my own place before. Just deciding which corner to stack the bookshelf/boxes in seemed like more commitment than I could manage. I dragged the previous owner's futon into the middle of the bedroom, so it looked like a giant slice of soggy bread floating on the hardwood floor, and thumbtacked some of my more colorful T-shirts to the wall because I didn't have any posters. Without Johan bounding through the house, without Lilly's New Age fussing, I did what I wanted: sang songs from *A Chorus Line* in the shower, ate tacos for breakfast and Pop-Tarts for dinner, used the backs of chairs to hang my clothes. It was nice never having to wait for the toilet or search for a clean glass in someone else's filthy dishes.

There was just one problem. I couldn't sleep. At first, I thought it was the oddness of being in a new place. I bought some cheap shades to block the eastern exposure, and went to bed wearing my favorite sleeping outfit, the University of Ohio nightshirt Jimmy had given me as a good-bye present. Kalia came over and smudged the apartment with a wizened bunch of something that she said was sage but which smelled exactly like pot. She suggested I move my futon ninety degrees and sleep facing north. But nothing worked. Whenever I tried to sleep, I would see Esto's sad yellowed eyes, like dull coins in the crinkled purse of his face, and then I'd start wondering if I should have done something sooner, tried to intervene. Who would I have called, though? A therapist, a cop, the SPCA? And to say what? My housemate drinks half-gallon bottles of Chianti, stockpiles evaporated milk, and tortures the cat? Who exactly was responsible in a case like this?

I kept reeling the whole scenario around in my head, and in the soft margins around midnight and at dawn, my visions of Esto would melt into an image of my father sipping delicately from a mug of coffee, then hurling it to shards on my parents' kitchen floor. Cloud's wails segued into my mother's sobs. I was on the sidewalk, clutching my sister's hand and waving as two different cop cars drove our parents away. Except sometimes in the dream, it was two hearses, and my sister's hand would disconnect from mine as she sped on her Rollerblades toward the expensive side of town. Then I'd wake myself up with these pathetic gasps, like a cat trying to heave a fur ball.

"It's only a dream, Linden, only a dream." I actually said that out loud while giving myself awkward pats on the shoulders to make my breathing slow down. I started to dread going to sleep at night, because the dream always came back. I did anything to stay awake—picked the former tenant's cats' hair off the futon with a strip of masking tape, recaulked the shower, cooked huge pots of vegetable soup and gave them to my landlady.

Everyone at work started to wonder what was wrong with me. I had oyster-shell shadows under my eyes. I flinched every time a phone rang, and I picked at my cuticles till my fingers oozed little serifs of blood. Finally, Sue cornered me in the staff lounge. "I'm taking you out for a drink tonight, and you're going to tell me what's up. You're four years too young for a Saturn return, and PMS doesn't last this long. After work, McClanahan's, on Twelfth. Got it?"

She touched me on the shoulder, and tears blurred my vision. Sue looked like an actor in one of those Hallmark commercials; I'd heard the photographers smeared Vaseline on their lenses to get that weepy, soft-focus ambience. But my tears were real. I'd been half afraid of and half in love with Sue since the first day, enamored of her tough-guy stance and her nervous habit of doodling elves on the corners of her file folders. Receiving a tender gesture from her was like finding a five-dollar bill scrunched behind a seat on the bus: You could be glad, but not too glad, because the universe offered up such kindnesses only once in a long while, and you'd probably never be this blessed again. The attention made me feel guilty and grateful, flattered and seasick, all at once.

At McClanahan's, I fidgeted while Sue went to get our drinks. I spun the beer mats on their edges, like hula hoops. I struck matches and blew them out. I dumped salt in the middle of a cocktail napkin and rolled it up like a joint. When I looked up, Sue was carrying two glasses of ale back from the bar. The beer was pecan-colored, with creamy caps of foam. Sue walked toward me, holding the glasses out from her body almost reverently, biting her bottom lip in concentration. Then she stopped, noticed she was being watched, and looked at me. Her eyes were cactus green, with golden spikes shot through the iris, her hair a thatched roof of straw threaded with silver.

I'd been watching her since my first day at the shelter—the way she got right to the point on the phone with cops and district attorneys; the way she drank her coffee black, with exactly one and a half packets of Sweet 'n Low; the way she communicated with her hips like deaf people spoke with their hands, semaphoring meaning with the angle at which she stood, punctuating the message with wide belts, close-fitting pants. I imagined I was beginning to learn the code: Come here; don't bother; I want; I won't.

We drank our beers and discussed work stuff, like whether it was ethical to counsel an abusive husband and his partner at the same time, or whether the man and woman should always get separate sessions. About the ninth time I started to roll up my paper-napkin joint around its stash of salt, Sue put her hands on the table and slid the napkin away from me. "Okay, time to talk," she said. And left her fingers there, stopping mine in their tracks, while I told her everything.

I mean everything. My parents and their fights, my sister and her stock portfolio, leaving Baltimore, having sex with Jimmy and Chazz and the others, the fire in the yard and all the weird things Esto started doing, and then finally that last day, with him so naked and pathetic on the front porch before the cops took him away. How I'd stood there on the sidewalk feeling like I was the one who was naked, ashamed in front of everyone because I hadn't been able to stop things from getting that bad. There was one moment when Esto had stopped flailing and his eyes hunted for mine, his eyes like mouths pleading, *Help, help,* and I looked anywhere—the rosebush, the cop car's headlights—because I had nothing to offer.

Sue made these *mm-hmmm* sounds and kept her fingers on mine, right-angled, so our hands looked like the lattice crust of a pie. It was warm in the bar, and I could feel sweat forming at all the places where our skin met. I had a crazy thought that when she finally moved her hands, to lift her beer or change the subject or pay the check, there would be a *sccttttccchhh* sound, like Velcro, as our moist skin peeled apart. So when she first moved her thumb, lifted it enough that I felt a kiss of cool air on my knuckle, then placed it down again, I thought she was trying to relieve the tension, break the seal. Then she did it again—raised her thumb, paused a second, two seconds, and placed it back down, moving it gently over the soft web of flesh between my thumb and index finger. In the flinch after she raised her hand, I felt chilled from the loss of heat, dizzy from the drop in pressure, and, in my head, I was already begging, *Put it back down oh please put your thumb back down.*

Linden, get a grip, I told myself. This is not lust; it's empathy, mentoring, comfort. But even while I was thinking that, I answered the weight of Sue's hands by pressing back, raising my knuckles into the pad of her palm casually enough that it could have been the involuntary tic of an extradeep inhalation, although it was actually a test—and that was when she opened her hand like a fan and lowered her fingers into the V's between my own.

I couldn't look down. I couldn't look at Sue's face, either, because I knew she'd see in a glance how confused and horny and excited I was, so I looked at my beer, at the piping on the waitress's rayon shirt, at the Amstel sign above the bar. Meanwhile, I babbled on about Esto and my parents and the dreams I'd been having, while for the next twenty minutes our hands carried on a conversation of their own, tucking and sliding and softly maneuvering over the table. We kept talking as if we were not in any way accountable for their actions. When Sue got up to pay the bill, I couldn't look at my own fingers, but hid them in the pockets of my jeans as if they'd just humiliated me in public.

The car seemed to vibrate, the way a concert arena does after a really vigorous drum solo, the kind you can still feel between your ribs ten minutes later. Everything I could think of to say was idiotic, so I didn't say anything. I noticed how Sue shifted gears, anticipating when the car needed to climb or slow down and slipping the gearshift neatly, casually, into its slot. I could feel myself blush, watching her. So I looked out the window. We were half a block from my house when Sue said, "Do you think you're responsible for Esto's drinking?"

"Responsible? Well, no, not exactly. I mean, I know it was his choice to drink. But I feel bad that I didn't say something earlier.

I don't know. Maybe I could have talked him into going for treatment."

Sue was smiling and shaking her head no in a way that completely unnerved me. Or maybe it was the way she was driving with one hand and had the other slung across my seat, her fingers drawing orbits in the short hairs on the back of my neck. "You couldn't have saved him. There's something he needed to learn from all this, some lesson. There are no accidents in this world, you know. And you can't save people. I learned that a long time ago in this business."

She turned off the car and moved her hand from my neck to my thigh. "Back there in the bar—did that feel as good to you as it did to me?"

"I don't know. I mean, yes, it felt good. But I wasn't sure if—I wasn't sure how you meant it. Like if you were just being friendly or what . . ."

Sue's laugh had a coarse, mustardy edge. "When I want to be friendly, Linden, I *shake* hands. That was definitely something else." Then she leaned across my seat and kissed me. Not methodically like Jimmy or reverently like Chazz. Sue's kiss was hooked as a question mark, definite as a dare. Her tongue was quick, a lizard's dart in and out of my mouth, my ear. She licked her way down my neck, unbuttoned my top button with her mouth.

"Come over here," she said, leaning out of her own seat and arching toward mine. We both giggled as she crawled over the gearshift, accidentally kicked open the glove compartment, then nudged it closed with her hip. But then she was kneeling over me, straddling my lap, and there was nothing lighthearted about the way her lips zeroed in on mine.

Even then, I could see the modus operandi unfolding, going

back to that moment in the restaurant when she lifted her thumb and made me wait just a second too long, made me ache and doubt, before answering my prayer with a yes. I had a glimpse of how this would go. Just as I was finding myself—contrary even to my own flimsy code of sexual ethics—French-kissing my boss in the bucket seat of a Honda, I could imagine myself stepping further and further over the line, sneaking flowers onto her desk at work and enjoying the lie she'd tell about where they came from, making out hotly in the supply closet, going to bed with her while her partner flew to a nursing conference in Wichita. And all the while feeling not quite responsible for my actions. Because she would always make the first move; I would not have to ask. Nor would I say no, even if I thought I should. And Sue's job was not to save me.

"What are you doing Saturday?" she asked into my ear.

"I don't know. Laundry."

"Maybe I'll come over and help you fold clothes. I'm good at that. Good at unfolding them, too." She swung her left leg over me and settled back into the driver's seat. "It all depends on whether I can get away. You know, the home scene."

I didn't want to know, didn't want to think about Sue's partner, Vicki, waiting at home with a cup of cold chamomile tea, already suspicious—or worse, not suspicious at all, but sleeping on her side, her hand straying over to Sue's side of the bed, while Sue clicked the lock softly behind her, pulled off her boots, and left them in the hall before cat-walking to the bedroom, thinking how delicious the dark was, and how she could get away with anything.

That's how my affair with Sue began. *Affair*—that word belonged in an era with seamed stockings and vodka gimlets. But *affair* was the only word that even came close—the word I had always applied to that cocktail of knowingness and shame, ever since I'd first heard my dad try to brush his teeth quietly at 2:00 A.M., then faked sleep when he tiptoed in his socks past my open door. By breakfast time, I could convince myself that everything was normal, that I didn't know what I knew, that all mothers wept over their Rice Krispies and all fathers packed a change of underwear into their briefcases.

Now I was the one having the affair, making love with my thirty-eight-year-old boss on my futon in the late afternoon, then napping alone on sheets that smelled of clove oil—Sue's signature perfume—and sex. Later, I'd eat granola on the fire escape and flip through *The Oregonian* as if nothing unusual was going on at all. Anyone who'd read even a little pop psychology could have diagnosed a whopping case of denial, but I'd sit there reading about the riots in South Africa and the land mines in Burma and thinking how, all over Portland, there were people reading the same tragic stories who would, in a minute or so, get up, put the paper in the recycling box, and go microwave some Lean Cuisine. As if those people across the globe were not their human cousins, as if those photographs didn't affect their appetites one tiny bit.

I thought maybe denial was nothing new, that it had probably been around ever since the first *Homo sapiens* heard a crunching sound in the bushes and thought, Nah, that can't be . . . just minutes before becoming that day's blue-plate special. Maybe evolution had just perfected a primal reflex, given the species centuries of practice at denial and all its relatives: pretense, ignorance, naïveté, and hope.

How else could I read *The Oregonian*'s front page, stare into the

eyes of a girl in El Salvador with a bloodied shoulder and hair the
exact color of mine, and not feel shredded with grief? So many
things that used to be secret weren't anymore: civil rights leaders
cheating on their wives, death squads making people disappear,
middle-aged men getting drunk on jug wine in the afternoon.
Maybe the human spirit just isn't big enough to contain all the
pain and hurt there is to know about. Maybe if we acknowledged, every single morning over breakfast, all that is rotten and
secret and painful and wrong, our tiny, frail minds would explode
and we'd end up muttering senselessly on street corners. Maybe
denial is the thing that keeps us sane.

That's the sort of thing I pondered while I became an expert
at not sleeping and waited for the whole thing with Sue to crash
and burn. It happened pretty much the way I might have
guessed. But first it lasted a long, fierce month. She'd call me from
a phone booth, usually on a weekend afternoon, and ask what I
was doing. "Not too much," I'd say, and then she'd ask if I wanted
company, and I'd say sure, trying to keep my voice noncommittal.
The first few times she came over, we made a point of doing
something social first, like drinking coffee or looking at my pictures of Yosemite or watching half an hour of TV. But soon we
just took the shortest path between two points, a swift and
breathless line from doorway to bed. Sue's lovemaking was delib-
erate, a bit triumphant; she'd lie back after making me come, a
look of pleased exertion on her face. Any minute now, they'd be
handing her the gold medal for sexual diligence. And me, well,
mostly I stayed on the receiving end, greedy for what I already
knew was scarce: She wore her watch to bed and never stayed the
night.

The best part was right after sex, when she leaned her head

on my chest and I pulled my fingers through her hair, smoothing it, and we talked in low voices that made me feel ticklish and lucky.

"You're brave," she told me once.

"I am? How?"

"Moving out here, all alone, leaving everything familiar, following your heart." She gestured toward our naked bodies, meaning, *this*.

"Doesn't feel brave," I said. "Feels like an accident, like I took a couple of blind turns and this is where I ended up."

"No, you had your eyes open," she said. "There are no accidents, Linden. No mistakes." I wanted her to say it again, that I was brave and wise and had my eyes wide open and was exactly where I was supposed to be. If she said it enough, I could begin to believe it. But I couldn't ask. I let one hand drift over her belly, and she moved it purposefully down. "Come here," she said, and slid on top of me. I closed my eyes.

Later, she'd zip her jeans and tuck in her shirt while I stayed on the futon, suddenly stricken with modesty, the sheet drawn up to my shoulders. "Gotta get back to the home front," she'd say. Home front, like it was a war. After she left, I'd lie there and watch David Letterman, moving my hands over my own body and feeling surprised by its hollows and protruding knots of bone. Is that how I felt to other hands?

Sometimes, a day or two later, I'd catch a glimpse of myself in the plate glass of a restaurant or store and feel oddly surprised to recognize the image, as if sex with Sue ought to have changed me in some plainly visible way. Affair, I'd think, I'm having an affair. But the picture that word conjured never really included me or the facts of what Sue and I were doing. I didn't know a word for

147

it—and without a word, even a word that is never spoken, my actions seemed not to exist. There was no one around to witness, to pretend sleep while Sue locked my door with the key I'd given her, no one even to withhold judgment. No one judged, because no one knew. That's how much I'd managed to secede. That's how alone I was.

It was exactly twenty-six days from our first kiss until Sue called me one Saturday afternoon and asked me to meet her at the Sizzler on Grand Avenue. I could tell from her voice—the same buttoned-up tone that she'd used to introduce herself at that first staff meeting—that our days of sleeping together were done. I could have made it easier for both of us. I could have said, Hey, that was really great while it lasted, and now we'll just go back to working together, right? No hard feelings.

But I didn't. Instead, I followed my "oh what the hell" impulse to make an awkward situation even worse. It was part plain revenge—I didn't want to let Sue off the hook that easily—and part perverse curiosity, like when you can't stop niggling at a painfully loose tooth, or when you're trying to get your own splinter out and you dig the needle in too deep, just to see how it feels. I wanted to know how far I'd fallen, and I'd never tell unless I learned how it felt to smack the ground.

So, in my best imitation of soap-opera sultriness, I said, "Sizzler? Wouldn't you rather come over here and indulge a different kind of appetite?"

There was a pause. I imagined Sue shifting emphasis from one hip to the other, measuring out the benefits and risks of one more fuck. Some large vehicle in need of a muffler job roared past her phone booth.

"What?" I shouted.

"I said, I thought it'd be nice to, you know, go out for a change. My treat."

"Okay," I said. "Okay. I'll meet you there in half an hour."

We stood in line behind a silver-haired couple, both of them stocky as hydrants. He wanted the Salisbury steak. She said no, that's what gave him the heartburn last time, and she wasn't going to be kept up all night running for the Rolaids. He said it wasn't the Salisbury steak; it was that Eye-talian dressing that didn't agree with him.

"I say play it safe, Murray, and get the salad bar. It's a better bargain, and besides, all the magazines say we need more roughage."

"I get enough roughage dealing with you," Murray muttered.

His wife socked him in the arm.

"Ow! Look at this—look how she treats an old man," he said to no one in particular. When it was their turn at the register, he ordered two Salisbury steaks and two salads. She paid, fishing the bills out of a flowered purse.

Sue poked me as the couple trudged off with their plastic trays and their number—23—on a little wire stand. "Happily ever after," she whispered.

"The joys of married life," I whispered back, and watched her smile reflexively, then lose the smile as she remembered why she was here, what it was she had to say to me.

I ordered the salad bar—even though I tended to agree with Murray: I had plenty of roughage just dealing with my life. I took a large plate and piled on iceberg and romaine lettuce, sliced cucumbers, shredded zucchini, hard-boiled egg, those phony bacon bits that smell like gerbil bedding. My salad teetered dangerously; three cherry tomatoes rolled down the pile and careened around my tray like billiards. Sue watched me heap stuff on with a worried, lip-biting look.

This time, she was the one fidgeting, pushing her broiled chicken around on the plate, raking patterns through the rice.

"So," she said. "Been having a good weekend?"

"Mm-hmm," I said around a big mouthful of lettuce. "You?"

"Yeah." She unfolded her napkin and laid it over her dinner as if she were tucking it in for the night. "A good weekend. Listen, Linden, I've been doing a lot of thinking and talking with Vicki. We're in a new place together, I think, really a deeper place, and I feel a new level of commitment. I think . . . I think sleeping with you was kind of a mistake. Anyway, I need to stop. It's not what I want to be doing anymore."

"I, I, I, I," I said, continuing to eat my salad, jamming the fork into pieces of cucumber as if I had to tranquilize them before putting them in my mouth. "What about me? What about we— I mean us?"

"Come on, Linden, you may be young, but you're not stupid. There was no 'us.' Okay, maybe I was in it selfishly, as a way of acting out or upsetting Vicki, or whatever, but you were in it for yourself, too. For the sexual experience. For the thrill of it, being a bad girl, playing on the edge. Right?"

"No. Wrong," I said, but I couldn't say how, because there were suddenly ropes of tears swelling in my throat. I couldn't explain to Sue that, for me, sleeping with her was different from sleeping with Jimmy and Chazz and Michaelangelo and Kalia and the rest. Those were for the experience, the "what the fuck" careless-ness of it; the sex helped distract me from myself. But with Sue, it

150

was the opposite. I was trying to get closer to something, not further away.

Sue reached out to put her hand on mine. I let her do it for a minute, let her think she could give me an instant of comfort, that this mess could be so easy to repair.

"There are no mistakes," I said. "No accidents. Remember?" Then I pulled my hand away, and it was smooth, no Velcro *scctttttccchhh*. Not any sound at all. That's how easily we came apart. And I saw how stupid I'd been, no matter what Sue said. It was no different from home—everyone for herself or himself. My sister and her Yuppie acquisitions; my dad and his mistress; my mom and her migraines and vision of the perfect marriage. Me and my running away.

I didn't know how to stop what I'd started, though, and I wasn't about to sit there in Sizzler with tears dripping down my face. So I mumbled a wet "Thanks," pointed vaguely at my salad, stood up, and walked through the restaurant, out the glass door, out of the air conditioning into a punch of September heat, then crossed the parking lot and just kept going.

I walked up Grand toward Broadway, the late afternoon gelatinous, like something I had to swim my way through. My lungs were clenched fists, the air threading in and out of my mouth in a clotted, wet string. I stopped to catch my breath and used my sleeve to sponge the tears that kept dribbling down my face.

Sue had said there were no accidents, no mistakes, that no one was responsible for anybody else. But that was bullshit. I'd seen the frozen look on her face, the way she pressed the phone to her head that day when Vicki fainted in Safeway and a doctor called from the emergency room. I'd seen her shake with rage and sorrow after hearing one of our clients tell a long, breathless story about her boyfriend and the roast chicken that came out burned, accidentally, and how what happened next was an accident, too, lifting her sleeve to show the red welts where she'd fallen against the radiator. I'd watched Sue wrap an arm around a sobbing woman's shoulder seconds before putting her in a taxi to go to the shelter at the YWCA.

Maybe that business about not being responsible was a story Sue told herself so she could feel okay about how much she *couldn't* fix, so she could make peace with all the women who left the YWCA after two nights and moved back in with the men who'd hurt them, suitcases in hand, black eyes turning mottled and yellow.

My tears were starting to slow down, but my face felt marked and swollen. I still couldn't take a whole breath without gasping. I walked slowly, just in case Sue might have second thoughts and come racing out of Sizzler to find me. But I wouldn't look back over my shoulder to check; I refused to be caught caring that much.

No mistakes, she'd said. But what about sleeping with me? That seemed like a mistake, a capital *M* mistake, no matter how you sliced it. My screwup as much as her own. Even though I wasn't the one breaking a pledge, even though there wasn't any precise transgressive label I could place on my shoulders, I still felt hot and shamed. Connie and I used to make up mean rhymes about the woman our father was having the affair with. Her name was Regina, but we pronounced it "Re-gyn-a" so it would rhyme with *vagina*. I wondered if she felt blameless, disconnected

152

from our confusion and our mother's pain, or if she squirmed under an itchy sense of misgiving, the way I squirmed to think about Vicki now.

Shit. I'd come to the other side of the country to get away from all that—the heaviness and the worry, the shouting and the anxious, drumming heart, the guilt and smallness I felt next to a whole line of mistakes. My grandmother and my mother had gotten linked up with the wrong people, and the city I lived in then was literally coming apart: The week before I left Baltimore, a rat fell through the ceiling of one of the elementary schools onto a second grader's desk. I couldn't even imagine the horror and betrayal; there you are, seven years old, one minute with your spelling book, learning how to make things plural by adding *s,* and next minute there's a rodent squirming in a rain of plaster dust on your desk, and all the kids are screaming and running away, like it's you who did something wrong. How could you deal with that?

I saw the ways people learned to manage—adults, anyway. If they could afford it, like Connie, they bought insulation, filled their world with a wide, beeping buffer of digital watches and answering machines and VCRs, teak miniblinds at the windows and enamel pots bubbling with imported tortellini on the stove. They stayed so busy and focused, they didn't have time to feel. And my parents—well, that was a different kind of self-absorption and escape, the endless wringing away at a relationship that had had all the life squeezed out of it years ago.

I'd had this idea that I could slip away, snap all the ties and be free. That I could find a place where people treated one another with benevolent laissez-faire: You do your thing, however strange and nonconformist it might be, and I'll do mine. That it might be

153

possible to live that way in a city too young to have accumulated generations of trauma, a place where people started fresh and didn't make the same mistakes.

For a while, I thought I'd found it. People on the West Coast *were* nicer, calmer, less driven. Nobody scolded me about my hair or my bank account or my sex life. And, in turn, Esto's drinking didn't have to be my problem. No accidents. No spills to clean up, because they were all meant to happen. But if that was true, why couldn't I let go of the twisted sensation I'd had the day the cops took Esto? Why couldn't I stop thinking about Cloud that night she had smashed Esto's bottles, frozen in the middle of her father's glittering debris? Another wave of tears, like the after-shock from an earthquake, rolled out of my eyes. Sue wasn't com-ing. I was on my own.

Cars streaked up Grand Avenue; on the left, some slowed to go over the Broadway Bridge, and others crawled in and out of park-ing lots: Sizzler, Tony Roma's, Baskin-Robbins. It was one of those weird stretches of city block that could be anyplace—Milwaukee or San Antonio or Portland.

I didn't want to see a Baskin-Robbins on the West Coast. I wanted there to be just one—the Baltimore store where I ate my first cone of cherry vanilla. I was three, and I didn't know you had to lick your way around. I ate from one side of the ice cream only, while the other side melted and slipped down my hand and into the sleeve of my blue sweater.

Connie was seven and in charge of us that day. She scolded me all the way home. When we got there, and our parents were shouting behind my mom's study door, Connie made me take off my sweater so she could wash it in the dishwasher. The washing machine was in the basement and too high to reach. Of course, soapy blue fuzz stuck to all the silverware and plates when the cycle was done.

I didn't really remember the incident, but Connie had told it to me enough times that I thought I could taste the creamy pinkness on my tongue, feel the ice-cream drips as they pasted my sweater sleeve to my arm. I used to think it was a story about Connie's superiority: I made a mess, and she tried to clean it up. Or about misplaced blame: Connie got in trouble for getting lint all over the dishes, even though I was the one who'd dripped the ice cream. But now I saw something else in the story, the other characters, whose absence made the whole incident possible— our parents, who had vanished into another of their fights, leaving a seven-year-old to baby-sit a three-year-old, then getting angry when we couldn't stay perfectly out of their way.

Maybe Connie told that story so often because she wanted me to know there was a time—one afternoon at least—when she did try to take care of me and got rewarded for her efforts with a smack on the hand and no ice cream for a month. Maybe that's when she decided her job was to stay out of reach. It wasn't too many years after that when she started baby-sitting for the Fiskers' kids, for $1.50 an hour, and opened her first bank account, dragging me along and showing me the different colored slips for withdrawals and deposits, candy green and yellow like Monopoly money.

At Broadway, I had a choice: left, over the bridge, or east, past car dealerships and used-furniture stores. The bridge looked immense and a little frightening, as if I'd need some special equipment to traverse all that metal. At Coliseum Ford, multicolored balloons were tied to the antennas of every car; they bobbed and strained in the wind. The sight was so incongruously festive—American cars with scowling bumpers parked under the happy tumult of the balloons, like a bunch of Methodist deacons at a children's birthday party.

When I was a kid, I used to imagine getting enough helium balloons to float away. "How many would it take," I'd ask Connie, "twelve, fifty, a hundred?" And she, already a pragmatic fifth grader, would say, "It doesn't matter—if you got enough to lift you off the ground, they'd pop from the pressure as soon as the air got thin." I never learned enough science myself to know if Connie was right, but that wasn't the point—it was too late; she'd already punctured my dream of flight.

I headed east. Behind me, the sun was low, sending bronze planks through the streets, making everything precise and dressed up—the leaves shiny green on top, turquoise-black underneath. I was hungry. It was seven o'clock, two hours since my manic grazing episode at Sizzler. I foraged in all my jacket pockets—two dollars and seventy-one cents. Great. I toyed with possible menus: a Big Gulp and a Tootsie Pop; a Häagen-Dazs bar and a piece of Bubble Yum; a microwaved burrito and a ginger ale. Nothing sounded good. I wondered if Sue had gone home and eaten a second dinner with Vicki. Did they make love first? Were they now in sweats, barefoot in the kitchen, talking quietly while one of them boiled water for rigatoni and the other tore up Boston lettuce for a salad?

Maybe there was more money in my pants. I reached into the left rear pocket, and my fingers closed around a stiff square. I pulled it out: the picture of Cloud I'd swiped from Esto's room.

As I waited for the light to change, I looked at the picture more closely and saw something I hadn't noticed before. In the open palm of Cloud's right hand was a small green caterpillar, no bigger than a squirt of toothpaste. The kind of caterpillar I used to trap in Maxwell House coffee cans, holes poked in the lid, furnished with what I thought was a lavish caterpillar suite of sticks and leaves. My caterpillar would spin its cocoon, and then I'd wait, whispering through the airholes about how great it would be when it came out as a butterfly. Every time, though, the white cocoon turned gray, then shrank and withered.

Cloud must have been fourteen when the picture was taken. She'd already identified her mother's dead body. But she cupped that caterpillar like a secret, her head bent not away from the camera, as I'd first thought, but toward that wiggle of green, a bug that would, she was sure of it, be saved by love. That was two years ago—before she watched her father vanish into alcohol and rhetoric, before she had to live with a bunch of weirdos. Including the one who left without saying good-bye. That last morning, my boxes loaded in the trunk of my car, I had stood outside Cloud's bedroom door for an endless minute, then slung her mother's poncho over the knob and tiptoed down the stairs.

I should return the picture; it wasn't mine, and Esto had already lost enough. There was a Quik Print across the street. I could make a copy of the photo, then mail the original back. Inside the store, an employee so springy that he must have been mainlining No-Doz accosted me as I reached for a copy key. "Hi! Anything I can help you with today?"

"Nope," I said, and headed for the copier in the far corner. I laid Cloud's picture facedown on the glass. There was Esto's hand again, the blocky epitaph: "August '83. Celine gone. Now what?"

I still had my hand on the picture, and the copier lid up, when I pushed the start button. The camera shuttled left, then right, the light snapped in my eyes, and a gray-and-white-image slid out.

There was Cloud, head tipped toward her hands, and the grainy image of my own fingers curled around the photo's edge.

"Helps if you close the lid." I looked over; three kids were clustered around the next copier, jostling one another to get at the panel of buttons. They were two girls and a boy, old enough to be in college but dressed like cast members from a touring company of *Godspell*—pants chewed off midcalf, dresses that looked like bedspreads, Jesus sandals, the girls' hair in knots.

"Do it bigger. Try one hundred and twenty-eight percent," one of them suggested.

"No," the other girl responded. "I want it to be subtle." I watched while a piece of paper with the words *swimming, helping, fucking, dancing, being, eating* came out of the machine. "See, look," she said, cutting the words into strips and holding *swimming* by one end against her collarbone. "I'll tie little strings to them, like this, and pin them on me. I don't want them any bigger." She grabbed a stapler and started attaching words to her skirt. "Make me another copy, for the real thing."

Her friend pushed the button, shrugged, and took a pair of scissors from the little tray of office supplies the Quik Print people provided. Then she began snipping holes in her Reed College T-shirt.

They noticed me staring.

"Halloween costumes," said the one with the words. "I know it's not for five weeks, but we have midterms between now and then. She's going as the holes in the safety net," and she pointed at her friend, who was struggling not to pierce herself with the scissors. "Guess what I am?" She picked up *helping* and *eating* and held one to each breast like pasties.

"Jesus, you don't even know her," growled the guy.

"Get a life, Thomas," she said. "No, really, guess what I am."

"I have no idea."

"A dangling participle! Get it?"

"Yeah. That's pretty good."

She jerked her chin toward the guy. "He can't decide what to be. Esther and I think he should go as liberal guilt. He could pin buttons all over his coat, you know, like 'Save the Whales' and 'No Nukes Is Good Nukes' and 'McGovern for President.' "

"Who?" Esther asked.

"Never mind. Don't you think that would be awesome? We're into conceptual costumes. My freshman year, I went as a Freudian slip."

Esther started to tug on her hand. "Come on. I have to study for bio."

I followed them to the register. The dangling participle girl fished in a woven bag and pulled out a gold American Express card. "Here. I'll pay for all these. Or, rather, my stepdad, the original Toxic Parent, will." And she shoved the card across the counter. Suddenly, she swiveled around to face me.

"Do you want to come to our Halloween party?" she said. "You can. Non-Reedies are allowed. You gotta have a cool costume, though. Here"—and she tore a piece off the brown Quik Print bag—"I'm Crow. Crow Davis."

"Carla," stage-whispered the guy.

"And this is my housemate, Esther Moonchild."

"Fishbein," he muttered.

"And this is our alleged friend Thomas. Here's our phone number. Really, it would be totally cool if you came."

"I'll think about it," I said. Crow pocketed the AmEx card and steered her friends toward the entrance. My copy cost seven cents. I paid for it and followed them. Outside the store, a man in a patched green parka sat on the curb.

"D'you have any change?" he asked as Crow and her friends swung out the door. He smiled, showing a row of perfectly straight tobacco-colored teeth.

"Nope, we gave at the office," Crow said, and laughed. "Come on, you guys, let's get some Ben & Jerry's pops at Safeway before we go back to campus. My treat." And they skipped off, arm in arm in arm.

"Okay, God bless you, miss," the man said, but Crow and her friends were across the street. Crow still had words stapled to the rear of her dress. *Fucking* and *being* flapped in the wind. I dropped ninety-three cents into the man's chapped palm. Dull grin of gold: a wedding band on the fourth swollen finger. "God bless, God bless," he said.

I was back at Broadway, and I decided to walk across the bridge after all. What the hell—it wasn't like anyone was waiting for me at home with a glass of wine and a rental copy of *Desert Hearts.* Anyway, I felt pulled toward the city skyline, its clusters of lights flirting with the river like the two of them had some big joke, the river winking back. A kind of Oz, and I had felt like Dorothy when I first got to Portland—the brick pavements, the pint-sized blocks, the sweet composty smell I couldn't name until someone told me it was from Weinhard's brewery. One breath of that dirty perfume could zip me right back to my first weeks in town, before Esto and Cloud and Sue, before everything got so complicated.

Tonight, the smell off the river was damp and mildewy. The temperature had dropped as soon as the sun set behind the West Hills, and blue-black shadows lounged on the concrete walkway.

Halfway across the bridge, I stopped and looked down at the water, simmering black. Cars rushed past me, their headlights a blur. The metal grating wheezed under my feet. Downriver, the Burnside Bridge lifted to let a boat through. It was one of those giant entertainment cruisers, a stern-wheeler made up to look old-fashioned.

As it glided closer, I could see there had been some kind of party on board—there were streamers tied on deck, balloons, and a huge arrangement of flowers. Most people were inside now, dancing, except for a few couples pressed close to each other on the deck. Maybe it was a birthday, or an anniversary, or someone's retirement—one of those celebrations that make people feel their lives are all linked up together in the best way possible, that they are all dancing to the same essential tune.

I had a sudden urge to climb up on the wrought-iron side of the bridge and jump. Not to drown. But to leap off the edge, arms flung out, and land in the middle of that riverboat party. I'd sit for a second, dazed, and then someone with a kind face would say, "We've been waiting for you," hand me a plate of hot hors d'oeuvres, and lead me into a liquid waltz. It scared me, how much I wanted to leap, how desperately I wanted to land. I turned and ran the rest of the way across the bridge.

When I got to the downtown side, I stopped to lean against a building, curling my fingers around the crumpled dollar and coins in my pocket. My feet ached, I could feel the first sting of a blister from running in my sandals, and there were lumpy shadows gathering in the doorways. I started walking, fast, staying so close to the curb, I was almost in the street. But then I couldn't remember which direction was south, or where the light-rail stopped, or whether $1.71 would be enough for a ticket home.

I kept thinking of that man with the parka and the perfect ocher smile. My breathing began to slow down. He had been someone's kid once, a toddler with a runny nose and disheveled hair. Later, someone had loved him enough to slip that wedding band over his knuckle. So how did he end up at Eleventh and Broadway, begging change from spoiled Reedies? Where were the people who were supposed to care?

I crumpled Crow's phone number into the nearest trash can. I hated her, bounding across the street with Daddy's gold card in her bag and dangling participles flying from her ass. Never looking back to see what was hurt behind her. Even those names—Crow, Moonchild—as if they could reinvent themselves out here on the very edge of the continent, leave history to fester and seethe, and start again with no regrets. Except there were always regrets, missing pieces, mistakes. Swallowed losses that burned all the way down to your gut, and kept burning.

When I remembered Esto, I remembered his shredded yell the day the cops took him, and I remembered him shaking my hand the day I moved in, that warm cradle of palms. I couldn't untwist them: the gift, the loss. I didn't want to. Is that what it was like for Esto, after Celine killed herself—that every thought of her had daisy necklaces and Nembutal, desire tied up in numb knots of grief? You could squeeze your eyes shut on memories like that. You could be drowned by them, like Esto was. Or you could carry them in both hands: all the wanting, all the sheared and shattered pieces of survival.

At the next corner, I leaned on the walk button, as if some useful instructions might flash on the little sign. Instead, it was the usual stick-figure, stepping cheerfully ahead. You, too, Linden, I told myself. Left foot. Then right foot. Just get to Pioneer Square and you'll be okay.

When I first moved to town, Johan gave me a whole speech about Pioneer Courthouse Square, like he was on retainer from the Portland Chamber of Commerce, blabbing on about how it reminded him of the great European plazas and how I must, I really must, experience it. So I sat on the gritty bricks from seven o'clock one morning until the guy with the steam-cleaning machine blew away the last gum wrapper at 1:00 A.M. And I watched.

I stayed there all through the lunch hour, while businessmen ate their efficient sandwiches on the low, curving brick steps, rolling up their shirtsleeves and loosening their ties in a modest gesture of rebellion. Women sat with their stockinged knees pressed tightly together, trying not to get Thai peanut noodles on their dry-clean-only skirts.

In the middle of the square were teenaged boys with Hacky Sacks, antiabortion screamers with posters of bloody fetuses. Tourists wandered around the square's edges like they were waiting for an invitation. They oohed and aahed over every little thing—the street sign listing distances to Japan and the moon; the statue of the man hailing a taxi: the echo corner, where you could stand on a bronze disk and whisper, and your friend could hear you perfectly from ten feet away.

A car honked its horn at me so harshly, it sounded like a curse, and I almost fell off the curb as the driver took a wild right turn onto Morrison. Men in suits and women in dresses rustled past, heels ticking anticipation on the bricks, heading out of theaters, into restaurants. One more block. My stomach felt squeezed; my blister seared with each step. I practically limped across to the Broadway and Yamhill corner, where the light-rail stopped.

After dark, that corner of the square belonged to street kids: green hair and chains, pierced eyebrows, pet ferrets on leashes. I'd seen the kids try to sleep on benches or huddle against the fountain until a cop woke them and shoved them along. Sue had told me how they turned tricks and stole stuff and sold their own plasma so they could buy cigarettes and drugs. Some of them weren't even teenagers yet—boys with young, fluty voices and girls in spandex pants to accentuate the hips they didn't have—and I used to wonder where the hell their parents were, how large a crack there had to be in a family that a twelve-year-old could fall through it. Then I spotted one—a girl, maybe fifteen—with a baby she hauled around as if it were some irritating parcel, and I added on ten years and saw how life could unravel, how easily people peeled apart from one another.

Tonight, there were just a few kids, slouching in a smear of orange-yellow streetlight. One skinny, tall guy, all elbows and angles, in an army jacket with Greenpeace bumper stickers pasted to the back. A girl, maybe his girlfriend—shaved head, armful of studded leather bracelets, butterfly tattoo on her left shoulder. A kid with long, greasy black hair—I wasn't sure of the gender—leaning against the lamppost, reading a thick book. And a girl who stood apart from the others, peering up Broadway like she was waiting for a ride. Wearing hot pants and spike-heeled sandals, a halter top, her hair piled on top of her head and secured with a pair of chopsticks, dangly earrings that caught the headlights of passing cars and made it look as if she had tiny lighted birthday candles in her ears.

A blue Ford slowed at the light. The girl walked over, teetering a bit across the bricks, and said something through the driver's half-open window. Then she tipped her way around to the passenger side and got in, all before the light turned green. Just before she closed the door, she half-leaned out of the car and gave a little wave in the direction of the other kids. They didn't even look up. I felt sick—dizzy enough to sit down right there on the cold bricks. I drew my knees up, stretched my T-shirt down to cover them, and waited. Watched while the Ford swung a wide, reckless left on Yamhill and headed down toward the river. Where would he take her? I tried to picture the motel room, somewhere on Interstate Avenue, with a stained chenille bedspread and a crack in the mirror. Would she shut her eyes while he did it? Would he tell her his name? And afterward, in the car, the sticky bills clutched in her hand, would he feel satisfied or sad? Would she feel rich or broken? Once you'd come to that, disconnected so completely from yourself, how did you ever find your way back home?

The light changed its mind—red, green, yellow. Traffic pulsed and stopped. The tall, skinny kid zoomed his skateboard around and around in circles, trying to bug the one who was reading in the lamplight. The girl used a nail file to rip a new hole in her jeans. When I looked up, the blue Ford was back, idling at the corner. I heard shouts from inside the car; then a door opened and slammed again, and the driver squealed off. I watched the girl gather herself slowly to a standing position. Her halter was untied, and her breasts looked like egg whites, pale and shivering. Her shoes were gone. Barefoot, she picked her way across the street toward the square. When she got to the corner, close to the oval of orange lamplight, she raised her head. The light hit her hair all at once, made her a matchstick, her head aflame, and it was in that strobe of brightness that my whole body started to shake, and I recognized Cloud.

I took her home. Home to my apartment, that is, because when I asked her where she lived now, she shrugged her shoulders and stretched her arms toward the corner: Here. I live here.

"Okay," I said. "That's fine. But tonight, I want you to come home with me. Okay, Cloud? Okay?"

She nodded. I used my $1.71 to buy two tickets for the MAX train; when it came, I half-carried Cloud up the steps and eased her into one of the plastic seats. Her lip was bruised and puffy; there was a scribble of blood above one eyebrow. She swayed with the train's motion, and I put a hand on her shoulders to steady her.

"Cloud, what happened? Did he—how did he hurt you? If you want, you can press charges. The police . . ." She shook her head vigorously—at first an emphatic no, then a kind of manic shaking, as if she couldn't stop, and then she started to cry without out a sound, tears leaking noiselessly from her eyes, dribbling down to the shelf of her swollen lip.

"It's all right. You're going to be all right." I didn't believe it myself—at least, I wasn't sure if I believed it, but it seemed like an important thing to say. And the words soothed Cloud; she swiped at her eyes with her hand and nestled in closer to me. She smelled of sweat and beer, and just faintly of the lavender shampoo she used to use, back when we lived with Esto and Johan and Lilly.

"When we get home, you can take a bath, if you want. And I'll lend you some pajamas. And in the morning, we can figure out what to do."

Cloud nodded like a child, like she had no reason to doubt the truth and sincerity of what I was saying. Didn't she know I was making it up as I went along? Didn't she know I was petrified of each promise I made? A bath, pajamas, a bed of blankets made up on my couch, and then what? I had a brief urge to untangle my arm, push the button for the next stop, and tell Cloud it had been nice to see her again, but now, so long. I didn't, though. It wasn't guilt or obligation that kept me there. I knew I could walk off that train any second and leave Cloud to manage in whatever way she'd been managing before. No, what kept me was the way her shivering back fit the circle of my arm, the way I felt scared and solid at the same moment.

I sat on the train, listening to myself talk evenly into the snarl of Cloud's hair, talking us into the next day as if it were linked to this one in a sure, unbroken chain—"sleep, and then I'll make some coffee; we can sit on the fire escape and have bagels . . ."— letting the train's motion, a hunger forward, a soft lurch from side to side, rock us both back from the brink.

NERVE

Dark Is Not a Single Shade of Gray

About a million years ago, before Lettie Logan drove her Toyota into the Kern River near Bakersfield and drowned on the spot, I asked her daughter, Miranda, what went through her head at night before she fell asleep.

"Seals," Miranda said, her sibilant *s* rustling through her teeth like a cracked broom straw. I took that answer as one more sign that Miranda had inherited all of her mother's exotic looks and none of her insight.

I was eleven at the time and walked through the days with my heart unbuttoned, waiting for the world to flood in. Puberty, in a year or two, would clip the feathers of my wanting, narrow it into a fierce crush on Tommy Mandell, who would respond in due course with sweaty slow dances, abrupt kisses, and his silver ID bracelet, a Bar Mitzvah gift.

Later I would learn to mask my disappointments—in boys, as in other things—as a matter of survival. But at eleven I was impatient, restless, easily fed up. When I packed my nightshirt and toothbrush to sleep over at Miranda's, I imagined us having long whispered talks into the darkest part of the night. I lay in the upper bunk (Miranda was afraid of heights), ideas shuffling through my head.

"Hey, Miranda, what if each person has an exact twin somewhere in the world, living a totally different life but thinking all the same thoughts?"

"That can't be true," Miranda said. "We would have learned about it in science."

Or I'd say: "If you had a choice, would you rather be paralyzed or blind?"

"Neither one!" Miranda said. "Don't ask me such awful questions. Let's talk about something else."

I thought for a long time, watching the arcs the sheet made from my toes to my stomach to my shoulders. Then I leaned down over the lower bunk. "Well, what do you think about at night before you go to sleep?"

"Seals," Miranda whispered, then rolled on her side and pulled the sheet over her black hair.

Miranda had her mother's coloring—hair the bitter black of scorched wood; dark, deep eyes; skin light as skimmed milk, so pale that it looked almost blue in certain light. Miranda's mother, Lettie, rarely left the house. I thought it was probably because of her complexion—skin like that would burn bright red in fifteen minutes. We had learned in science about pigment cells and why some people don't tan.

When I suggested that to my mother, she just sniffed and said, "Lettie Logan is an odd one, you certainly have to say that." What do you mean, "odd," and *who* certainly has to say it, I wanted to know, but she just fed me more quotes of the day. "Lettie has always stepped to a different dance, that's all."

"Drummer, Ma. The beat of a different drummer." We had done Thoreau in advanced English.

Personally, I didn't see anything odd about Lettie, except that she was probably the least boring adult I knew. She read the entire *New York Times* every day, and *The New Yorker* and *National Geographic,* and tons of books, and she spent hours in the kitchen cooking food we never had at home.

My mother would say, "Here's your tuna casserole, honey." Or "I have to finish this grant, so would you put some potatoes in the oven?" At Miranda's house, Lettie paraded out of the kitchen, perspiring, her bangs pasted to her forehead in a charcoal fringe. She would serve everyone, saying, "Here are all the flavors of Madagascar," or "A nostalgic trip into the Old South, which survives in its robust cuisine."

And on the plates would be some delicious thing that looked like a painting and tasted like all the places I wanted to live. Sometimes we even had wine. When Miranda's father, Ted, wasn't home, that is. He was a police officer and didn't approve of eleven-year-old girls drinking alcohol. Neither did my parents, but I never mentioned that particular part of my visits to Miranda's.

Lettie taught me about wine—how to uncork a bottle of pinot noir to let it breathe, how to swirl my glass and look for tears streaking down the inside of the thin crystal. I loved the feeling of the wine, sweet edge and dark sour middle, going down my throat. Lettie sipped and poured and told stories about growing up in Avila Beach, all the strange people who lived there.

She told us about an old woman who grew sweet potatoes in stacks of old whitewall tires, about the man who went off to India, became a mystic, then came back and ate a bicycle to raise money for the grade school. People pledged a certain amount for each part he ate. My favorite story was about the twins whose mother named them Jake One and Jake Two, the numbers spelled out like middle names. They were gymnasts and led the town parade each year, doing perfect back flips down Third Street.

When Ted was home, we ate fast and silently and drank pink lemonade. He always sat to my left, still wearing his uniform from work, the powder blue shirt with sweat rings under the arms, navy blue polyester pants. He'd take off his revolver and put it on the sideboard, where they kept the mail. Lettie hated that. I could tell.

Miranda's little brother, Jeff, always begged his father to let him wear the badge. It was a star inside a circle and said T. H. LOGAN across the bottom. I used to make up things the T. H. might stand for. "Trigger-Happy" Logan. "Top Honcho" Logan. Or, watching Ted push curried vegetables into his mouth, "Totally Hungry" Logan.

On Jeff's eighth birthday, Ted did take off his badge when he sat down. He handed it over with a serious look, like he was passing me the crown jewels, and said, "Give this to my son, please." The badge was light, not solid, but a thin piece of metal, like something from a vending machine. I shrugged and gave it to Jeff, who stuck it on his T-shirt and beamed all through dinner.

Right after we sang "Happy Birthday," Ted had to go back to work. "We're down one man on the late shift, honey," he said. Jeff unpinned the badge and looked like he might cry. Miranda swallowed forkfuls of cake without seeming to chew them. I tried to catch Lettie's eye, but she was staring into her wine, swirling the glass, watching the tears.

Later that night, I lay in the top bunk listening to Miranda breathe. She carried her sibilant *s* even into sleep, exhaling with a small rustle. I imagined Miranda breathing the same little pocket of air, recycling it through her lungs her entire life, being satisfied with that.

She made me think of the six-celled creatures we looked at under the microscope in science, floating around, wanting nothing but survival. Miranda Logan is a simpler life-form, boys and girls, I said to myself, pretending I was Mr. Beame lecturing our sixth-grade class.

Then I felt mean. Miranda was my best friend—practically my only friend. She moved to town in fourth grade, when her family left the coast, and we'd been close ever since. I envied her black hair and smooth looks, the way she moved without seeming to try, noiseless. I was the opposite, always bumping my shins on the desk, getting stern looks for talking in class, asking questions that made adults squirm, roll their eyes, and finally say, "Because it just is. Can't you settle for that?"

At first I thought Miranda might be someone I could talk to, really talk to. I tried, asking questions, telling her what I dreamed at night, coming up with plans for the two of us to get jobs as deckhands and sail around the world. Nothing flashed back from her perfect pale expression. Mostly, she listened and smiled. And invited me to sleep over nearly every Friday night of our sixth-grade year.

That night of Jeff's birthday, I lay listening to her breathe, to the tick of rain on the Logans' wooden porch. Then I heard the back door open, pause, and fall shut with a heavy click.

From the window of Miranda's room, I could see into the backyard, the garden toppling to seed under a slender moon. And then Lettie, wandering through the yard like a stranger, fingering the shrubs, pressing her palms flat against tree trunks. I grabbed my robe, stuck my feet into sneakers, and walked fast through the Logans' silent house.

I stuck my head out the back door. "Lettie? . . . uh, Mrs. Logan? I couldn't sleep, and I saw you outside. Is everything okay?"

From across the yard, she waved to me, one thin arm in a billowy pajama sleeve. "I couldn't sleep, either," she said, "and the night reminded me of something. That sound the wind makes. I don't know. Maybe I just imagined it." In her other hand, the one that wasn't waving, she held a wineglass delicately by the stem, as if it were a rare flower she had raised to maturity. She took a long swallow, then licked the inside rim.

"Did Miranda ever tell you how we swam with the seals at Avila Beach?" she said. I went over and sat down next to her in the damp grass, gathering my robe over me like a blanket.

"When we lived on the coast, I used to go and watch the seals every day. Miranda, too. She could swim practically from the day she was born, and I . . ." She lifted the glass again, discovered it was empty, and giggled.

"The seals," I prompted.

"Yes. Well, we swam with them. An old fisherman taught me how. They're very smart, like children. Anyway, the key is not wanting too much. You just swim, feel the water pillow over and under you. Maybe you backstroke a little. You know where the seals are, but you don't . . . um, you don't . . ."

The wet grass was beginning to soak through my pajamas and robe.

"They'll swim to you if they know it doesn't matter. If you can keep from wanting it," she said. "There was one that loved me best. We were great friends."

Lettie stood up and began to walk a bit unsteadily toward the house. Halfway there, she tripped on one leg of her pajamas and folded over into the grass. I ran to help her up. She looked at me, and her face was bright and thin, a starved moon, her eyes huge as craters.

"I was in love with a seal. Ted was so jealous. He made us move inland; he made us leave. Do you think I'm crazy? My husband was jealous of a seal." And she started to laugh, her shoulders quivering under the pajama top. Suddenly, she stopped.

"Can you hear the ocean?" she whispered.

"No," I said.

"Neither can I. I used to, when we first moved here. Ted said I couldn't possibly, but I know I heard it. Waves smacking the shore. That whooshing, the bubbling underneath. Back and forth, like a conversation. One sound is the question; then the answers wash back.

"One night, I woke Ted and said, 'I can't hear the ocean anymore; I've stopped hearing it.' And he said, 'Good,' and went back to sleep."

Lettie reached into the grass and held up a corked bottle. "Let's drink to the ocean," she said. I took the bottle from Lettie and tilted it to my lips. Red wine filled my mouth, and a little dripped off my chin onto my nightshirt. It burned as I swallowed, made my eyes tear, and I suddenly thought of blood. I felt a little queasy. I took another sip, more careful this time not to spill it.

That's when the back porch light blasted on, a white scream into the yard. And suddenly, Ted was standing over us both, a dark barrel, still in his uniform. When he talked, it was the quiet, even tone that scared me, like someone measuring out precise amounts of poison.

"That's it, Lettie," he said. "What did I say the last time? You promised. Do you know what time it is? An eleven-year-old kid. Jesus Christ."

"Go to bed," he said, and it took a minute to realize he meant me. I ran back up to Miranda's room and lay there, listening as Ted's voice got louder and louder from the yard. A door shut with a crack, then the sound of dishes smashing to the floor, voices and cabinet doors and Jeff sobbing in the hallway, and finally another door slamming, angry and final.

I leaned down from the top bunk. Miranda slept right through, her black hair sleek in the light coming through the window, her breathing the only evenness in the house.

The next morning, I woke before Miranda and rode my bicycle home. My mother hugged me hard when I walked in. "You're okay?" she said, and I shrugged. "Of course I'm okay. Why are you acting so weird?"

Later, she told me she had talked to Miranda's father and they had decided it would be best for me not to sleep over there anymore. I started to shout. "Best for whom?" but my face felt hot and I just said, "Okay."

I did not sleep at Miranda's again, and my mother never mentioned that night. In junior high school, Miranda's graceful silence grew thick, like a gel. She joined no clubs, had no friends. I sat up front, answering all the social studies questions, trying to impress Tommy Mandell. It wasn't that hard.

At record hops the rest of that year, I tried to keep my mind still while Tommy and I shuffled in circles around someone's rec room. "A kiss for your thoughts," Tommy said now and then, planting his mouth on mine as if to stop a leak. I learned to keep my face unquestioning and my mind silent. I cultivated a look of satisfaction. Tommy was less trouble that way.

By the time I graduated from high school, I had acquired a reputation as someone to whom things came easily—ice-skating, calculus, a scholarship to the University of Vermont. I asked questions that had answers. I forgot there was another kind.

It was right before midterms my freshman year when my mother called to tell me about Lettie Logan. My mother said Miranda had been hospitalized—actually, several weeks before the accident. Miranda had finished high school, started a job at the county library, and then got fired. Apparently, she'd lost her temper and yelled at a man who was trying to renew a book, just started screaming and couldn't stop. So she checked herself into the psych ward at St. Francis.

"I think you should call her," my mother said.

My hands were sweating so hard when I dialed the number of St. Francis Hospital, my finger kept skidding off the button. I asked for Miranda.

"Hi. This is Beth. Remember me? Listen, my mom just called and told me about your mother's accident. I'm really sorry."

"It wasn't an accident," Miranda said. "She meant to drive into the river. She was plastered."

"Oh . . . well." I could feel myself about to babble, anything to fill the tunnel of quiet. "What an awful way to go, though. I always dreaded that happening when I learned to drive, going off a bridge or something. Always figured I'd roll down the window and swim out."

"My mother couldn't swim," Miranda said. In the crackling silence, I remembered that night with the wine, and Ted, and Lettie's story.

"Wait, Miranda, that can't be true. Your mother told me—"

"My mother was a liar and a drunk," Miranda said. "And my father was a bully. Did my mother ever tell you why he made us leave the coast?"

I had an urge to put down the receiver, clap my hands over my ears. But Miranda's words were the first white fingers of a tide, moving forward, inevitable.

"Ummmm . . . I don't quite recall. It was a long time ago." That was a lie; I remembered exactly the ribbons of Lettie's voice, the way she cupped her wine glass like a prayer, the wet, cold grass chilling through my pajamas. I shivered a little, holding the phone.

"My mother got her stories out of a goddamned bottle," Miranda said. "And you swallowed every single one of them. She poured and you drank. Well, I've got a shot for you. A good stiff one—ha!" And she laughed a low metallic laugh I'd never heard, like a bag of rusty knives.

"Avila Beach," she said. "I was eight. My mother practically lived at the ocean. As soon as we left for school—boom—there she went. With a bottle. To watch the seals."

"Right, the seals," I said a little too eagerly. At least Lettie hadn't made up that part. "She told me about that, how you two swam—"

"Do you want to hear this or not, Beth? Forget the swimming. My mother drowned, remember? *I'm* telling this story now.

"My mother just sat on those rocks and watched the seals. One in particular. She told me it asked her to come live in the ocean and she said she'd have to think about it. I hated that seal. It was trying to take my mother away.

"One day, I came home and my mother was in bed, not at the beach. My dad's police uniform was hanging, wet, in the bathroom. Red stains in the sink. And nobody saying anything."

She stopped talking, and I gripped the phone tighter, pulling it close to my head. What if Miranda was going crazy right this instant, slipping off the edge into silence or screams forever? "Hey, Miranda," I said quietly, a small thread to pull her back. "Tell me what happened."

"Ha!" she said. "They wouldn't tell me. Until the next day at school, when I heard people talking about the seal that had been killed. A seal came up on the beach, and some old lady got scared it was going to hurt her grandson. She called the police and told them there was a seal on the beach and it looked diseased. Said it was chasing a baby.

"My father was the cop on duty. When he got to the beach, there was a crowd around the seal. He pushed through with his goddamn gun up, and then he squeezed the trigger.

"The seal died right there in front of everyone. I heard it just shook and shook and then it stopped.

"Boom!" she said, suddenly too loud, then laughed her rusty laugh again. "End of seal, end of story. Mom stayed in bed with a bottle for two weeks. Then Dad announced he'd gotten a job in the Bakersfield cop shop. My mom cried, but I said I didn't care.

I knew every place would be just the same. So we moved. You know the rest—more or less.

"Listen, Beth, they want me to stop talking. They're always telling me that. It was nice of you to call." And she hung up.

I sat there with the phone in my hand for a long time before I put it back in the cradle. My throat burned, like too much red wine too fast. I wanted to scream, throw up, burst into tears. Instead, I put on pajamas and climbed the ladder to my bunk bed, crawled in, and pulled the sheet over my face.

That night, I dreamed I was dancing with Lettie Logan, dancing barefoot over wet grass in the moonlight. Then the sky split open like a mouth, and rain streamed down. The rain was sticky. I watched it splash red on my wrists. I hugged Lettie tightly. Her long black hair streamed over her face and mine.

"What do you think about before you fall asleep?" I asked Lettie in my dream.

"Not waking up," she said.

Lettie's hair was one long plane of wet, soft black, with a pulse everywhere I touched. The taste of salt. And then someone shouting "No!" and it was me, awake, tears burning my face, my hands open and clutching the air over my bed, trying to pull matter out of the darkness.

The Honor of Your Presence Is Requested

They had been down this street before. Glow-in-the-dark Santa on the corner lawn, sleigh hitched in a life-sized manger, the three Wise Men helping to unload gifts. If Zack had his camera, he would shoot it in black and white: Christmas-night tableau of suburban kitsch.

Look, he almost said to Rafi, Christians with a sense of humor. But he knew this was the sort of night when every conversation was built of slender glass rods. They would grope toward each other, break something in their clumsiness, try to gather the shards, and end up with blood on their hands.

Zack yanked the glove compartment open.

"Whoa, amigo. Be nice to Vinnie the Volvo. You want to keep him in good spirits so he'll take us to the beach, right?"

"God, I hate it when you call him—it—Vinnie. It's just a fucking car. And we won't ever get to the beach, at this rate. We're lost. It figures."

"It doesn't *figure*," Rafi snapped. "It's not divine punishment,

183

Z; it's not a sign of moral instability. We're just lost. It happens to people sometimes."

Zack reached for the map. He could see only as far as the Volvo's headlights, little megaphones of bright against the murk.

Fourteen hours earlier, Rafi drove from Providence to Philadelphia while Zack navigated. Rafi was goofy, cheerful, drumming his long fingers on the dashboard in time to "Wake Up, Little Susie."

"So I was wondering," he said when they got close, "what I will be this time—your roommate, your friend, your best bosom buddy—no, oopsie, better not say 'bosom,' it might give Mami and Papi the wrong idea."

"Don't start," Zack said. "First of all, Elizabeth's not my mother. And we've been over this. The born-again thing. My dad will start quoting Leviticus, and Elizabeth will just look stricken and pour another glass of scotch. Is that what you want—to be told you're an abomination on Christmas Day?"

"Okay, okay. All I'm saying is, it's not like they don't know. We've moved together twice, both our names are on the answering machine, and there's the way we look at each other. Christ, Z, anyone with eyes—"

"You think we still look at each other that way?"

Rafi glanced over: Zack's profile, like the contested border of a country, its juts and coves, full lips and pale, thick brows, the green-blue eyes that could hold a gaze longer than anyone, as if sheer endurance would enable Zack to see what others missed.

" 'That way'? Oh, ho, you mean *that* way. Yes, from time to time."

184

Three hundred and fifty miles later, they bowed their heads while Edward said grace over four lukewarm Swanson turkey dinners.

"*Gracias a Dios.* Amen," Rafi said, and peeled off the tin foil. "Elizabeth, this was a brilliant idea. Who wants to spend Christmas Day over a hot stove and then do dishes for two hours? This way, we can just be here and enjoy one another's company."

In someone else's mouth—Zack's own, for instance—the words would have leached sarcasm. But Rafi's face was guileless, friendly as a dahlia. He was unbelievable; he really expected to talk with them. Under the table, Zack jammed his heel hard on Rafi's toes. Rafi shrugged, as if it were an accident.

"Edward, here's something I've been thinking about," Rafi said, fork poised over the little compartment of cranberry sauce. "You know, I counsel these kids, and they're all from different places. Just in the first grade, I've got Lao, Filipino, Chinese, Korean, two Pakistanis, a Ghanaian, a Russian kid, and three who just got here from Guatemala, not a word of English. It's a public school, so I can't talk religion to them, and I agree with that. But it's so clear that they need to believe in something, need a way to navigate whatever chaos they've been through. I thought you might have some ideas. . . ."

"Excuse me," Zack said. "I need something. Upstairs."

Elizabeth's bathroom was a mess—little vials of foundation, nail polish, lip gloss toppled on the vanity in a dandruff of mascara flakes. He sat on the cushioned stool, made his thumbs and forefingers into right angles, a frame held a few inches out from his face. He would shoot it in low light, a silvertone print left grainy on purpose, title it *The Babel of Beauty.*

Zack had been doing that ever since he got his first Instamatic, at the age of eight. Framing his childhood between four out-stretched fingers: his mother, for weeks so lost that she could barely pack his lunch, suddenly industrious at 4:00 A.M., stacking sand-wiches she'd made of saltines and chocolate syrup. His father kneeling by the double bed, reading angrily out of the Book of Job while his mother stared expressionless from a twist of sheets. The place he and Edward took her eventually, jazz of shadows across the Georgian portico of the mansion turned mental hospital.

Through the door, he could hear the weave of voices below, the *ting* of silverware. Zack took the stairs slowly, looking at the framed prints hung there, pictures he'd given Edward and Eliza-beth over the years. Razor-wire fence outside Auschwitz, lacy coils on a claret sky. Pigtailed girl skipping rope in a glass-strewn lot—the same patch of broken ground where her older brother would be shot four days later. Zack knew how a picture could capture one second of stillness in a month of bedlam. "Beautiful lies," he called them. He straightened the frames on his way back to the dining room.

The night before, Christmas Eve with the Campos clan: castanet of heels on the foyer floor, backbeat of music, the women's apri-cot kisses on Zack's cheek, children tugging his sleeve, men pulling him into conversation: What did he think of the *arroz verde,* the Nixon biography, the Million Man March? And Rafi's mother, uncorking the wine, a teasing smile on her lips: "So tell me, Zack, when are you boys going to get married and make honest men of each other?"

It was all too palpable, too close. Rafi rolling around on the floor with his nieces and nephews, folding pirate hats out of yesterday's sports section. "Hey, Zack, we need someone to be our shipwrecked sailor so we can rescue you and make you join us in terrorizing the oceans."

"No thanks, I get seasick," Zack said.

"Oh, come on. We're socialist pirates, right, kids? We loot the yachts of filthy-rich CEOs and distribute the booty to struggling fishing villages. But first, we eat all the expensive imported chocolates. . . . Come play with us." Zack shook his head, backed into the kitchen for another beer.

Later, they both bared their teeth in the bathroom mirror, brushing fiercely. "Don't you get it?" Zack hissed. "You're an insider here. I'll never be."

"It might help if you tried." Rafi spit peppermint foam into the sink. "What do you want, Zack, an engraved invitation? Zachary Elliot Paulson, you are hereby invited to show up for the rest of your life. No guarantees. Regrets only."

Small fists pounded on the door. "Tio Rafi, I got to pee." That night, they lay back-to-back in one of two twin beds in Rafi's old room, each man spooning the chilly air.

Six weeks earlier. "You're going to regret this" was Rafi's reply when Zack first outlined the itinerary. Zack the engineer of emotion, Zack the photojournalist who could slither under the yellow police tape and position a perfect shot of the firefighter weeping in the charred doorway. "Here's the plan," he told Rafi. "Christmas Eve with your family in Providence, Christmas Day with my dad and Elizabeth in Philly, then a bed and breakfast in Cape May for my birthday."

"I don't think so, amigo. It's crazy; we'll kill each other," Rafi had said. But Zack had that locked-drawer look in his eyes.

"You don't give people enough credit," Zack said. It was the opposite of the truth. Rafi was the believer, the one who loved without judgment or limit. He, Zack, was the one who wanted people to be larger than themselves, but secretly expected them to be so much less.

August, three years before. The first time they met. A neighborhood council meeting, everyone brandishing their rage like small, sharp knives. Then a man came to the microphone, his caramel hands winging open, closed, as he talked. "I'm Rafael Campos, I'm a guidance counselor at Hoover Elementary, and I live on Olive Street. I think that when people steal your mail or slash your tires, they're trying to give you a message. Yes, it could be more articulate, but it's not. So what's the message? And how do we, as neighbors, want to respond?"

Zack pretended he was photographing for the *New Haven Advocate* just to get close. He never told Rafi the camera was empty.

Later that night, Zack's kitchen.

"What do you mean, 'no faggots on film'?" Rafi said. "What about *Philadelphia?*"

Zack snorted. "Sanitized gay culture for the masses. And have you ever seen a family so supportive?"

"Well, yeah. Mine. Okay, how about *Tongues Untied?*"

"Great film. Poetry on celluloid."

"Yeah, but who saw it besides other gay men?"

"Who cares? It was art, not outreach. I wanted to live in that film. Red wine?"

"Gives me a headache. Got any dark beer?"

"Just Corona. Or lime seltzer. Take your pick."

"I'll just have water." Rafi picked up a copy of GQ. "You *read* this thing?"

"I take pictures for that thing."

"Oh. Oopsie. Well, the pictures are the best part. Really."

Zack sliced a baguette and toasted it, brushed each slice with olive oil, spread on a film of pesto, a wheel of yellow tomato, a wafer of feta cheese.

"That looks gorgeous," Rafi said. "What is it?"

"Bruschetta."

"God bless you."

"Very funny. Here, taste."

Rafi bypassed the plate, kissed wet rosebuds down the side of Zack's neck. "I always wanted to make love with a man who could make bruschetta."

"You didn't know bruschetta from bratwurst until fifteen seconds ago."

"Mmmmm. *Delicioso.* Can we eat it for breakfast?"

Spring break, senior year of high school. Zack and Tina broke up over breakfast. Pete's Diner off the interstate.

Zack had picked Tina to be his lab partner because she was smart. Then it turned out they had everything in common: only children, divorced parents, grave doubts about the existence of a merciful God. They liked Buster Keaton, hated Led Zeppelin, thought Hemingway was a bully and a fake. Both their middle names were Alex. When they made love for the first time, on Valentine's Day, squeaking on the vinyl couch in Tina's rec room, Zack was surprised at how easily their bodies slipped together. All that locker-room talk had led him to believe some sort of struggle was involved.

"That was nice," Tina said uncertainly. "I mean, you smell nice. But the earth didn't move or anything."

"Me, neither. Maybe we should have paid more attention in health class. Hey"—Zack pointed at the stout water stain on the ceiling—"doesn't that kind of look like Gertrude Stein?" Tina agreed that it did.

Now, at Pete's Diner, Zack shredding his hotcakes with a fork. How to say it: I think I'm a homosexual. This can't ever work. Tina, I love you, but there's no, um, spark between us. I need friction. I need—no pun intended—someone who rubs me the wrong way.

Tina gulped her coffee, then said, "Zack? Bad news. Rolf Jensen—volleyball captain? He asked me to the prom, and I said yes."

"Rolf Jensen? What are you going to talk about with Rolf Jensen? You're nothing like him."

Tina put her hand on his gently. "I know. I think that's part of the appeal."

The question was, How did you know if your life was the one you were supposed to be living, or if you'd made a bad turn a few blocks back and ended up where you were by default? How did you know if you were being an honest man? There were so many other worlds you might have entered, that you could still enter—each of them just a membrane away. One step to the left or the right, one boundary breached or never crossed, and you could have become someone else entirely. You could be driving a Suburu with a sleeping toddler in the car seat and a woman so much like you, she could be your twin, reading Alice Walker poems out loud. You could be hugging the highway, alone in a silver Corvette. You could be crazy or sane. Or you could be here, lost in Camden on Christmas night, with no idea what the next moment was going to bring.

Rafi pulled into a 7-Eleven and gave Zack a little nudge. "Real men ask directions," he said. *"Comprendes?"* Inside, fluorescent lights and a relentless jazzed-up version of "Deck the Halls" yammered against Zack's head. He wandered up and down the aisles, searching for a clue. Tastykakes. He hadn't had Tastykakes in such a long time.

"Zack?"

He recognized her in a second. "Tina, what are you doing here? I mean, *how* are you doing? I thought you lived in Boston."

"I did, until a few months ago. I was married—I don't know if you knew—and now, well, I'm not. My folks moved to Jersey, and I'm back home with them for a while."

"Mom, can I get these?" A girl with a thin, serious face skipped up to Tina, holding a package of butterscotch Krimpets.

"This is my daughter." Tina put an arm around the girl's shoulder. "Julie, this is Zack. He's a friend of mine from a long time ago."

Zack used to fantasize that Tina had gotten pregnant on that Valentine's Day night, and that the fertilized egg would just incubate inside her until years later, when she'd give birth to a living emblem of their friendship. He could picture the three of them playing Monopoly, going to matinees, making brownies while "Free to Be . . . You and Me" played in the background. They'd float like an image on a gelatin print, an eternity of peaceable, quiet communion.

Beautiful lies.

Outside, Rafi leaned on the Volvo's horn.

"I've got to go," Zack said. "Good to see you, Tina. Enjoy those Krimpets, Julie. Your mom likes them with Nestle's chocolate milk."

"I know," Julie said. "Bye, Mom's old friend."

When Zack climbed into the car, he saw that Rafi had torn their one and only map into ragged strips and made a paper chain that arced from the steering wheel to the rearview mirror. He'd put a doughnut on the dashboard and was singing softly, *"Estas son las mananitas . . ."*

Zack reached across the seat, collapsed the distance between them. Rafi's hands in his hair, mouth on his mouth, his kiss insistent, then gentle: apology, demand, invitation, gift. A car pulled out behind them, clicked on its brights—a dazzle of exposure, flinch of clarity, then muddy again, Rafi's face a blur, so close that Zack could not tell whose breath was whose. The whole car a frame around them, a picture he'd stumbled into, a place he could keep looking for the rest of his life.

Rafi leaned back. "It's after midnight, buddy. Happy Birthday from Vinnie the Volvo and me. What took so long in there?"

Zack shrugged, lifted empty hands to find his lover in the shadows. "There was a line."

Good with Animals

Some of the kids in Clara Metcalf's third-grade class wanted to name the new guinea pig Pluto, or Snot, or Buster, but then Myra Ferris stood up and said, "Strawberry" in a voice clear as middle C. She had been looking at the guinea pig, its pale brown fur and tiny raisin eyes, when the word *strawberry* formed in her mouth, ripe and blushing as the fruit itself.

Mrs. Metcalf's eyes jumped open like window shades. Myra hardly ever talked in class. She was a bulky child with hair the exact color of shredded wheat. Sweet but slow, Mrs. Metcalf decided the first time she met Myra's perpetually moist gaze.

"Straw-berry," Mrs. Metcalf said, sucking the word down to its pulp. "That is a lovely name for a guinea pig. Much nicer than Pluto or Buster."

"What about Snot?" said Robbie Tupperman.

Myra sat back down. The heat of everyone looking at her made her forehead sweat. Under her folded arms, it was cool and dark. "Let's take a vote," Mrs. Metcalf said. "Raise your hands as I call out our choices. . . ." Myra saw bowls of fruit piled up behind her eyelids. "Sixteen . . . seventeen . . . eighteen. And the winner is . . . Strawberry. Well! Congratulations, Myra."

Myra sat up, blinking, as if she'd just walked out of a movie theater. Mrs. Metcalf flashed her a shiny smile, and Myra ducked.

After that, each Friday afternoon a different child struggled proudly out of the classroom with Strawberry's cage, an old picnic blanket thrown over it so the guinea pig wouldn't get scared on the school bus. Mrs. Metcalf went in alphabetical order to be fair. The first one to take Strawberry was Nina Adamson, who wore different-colored tights each day of the week. Then Teddy Bullock, who knew the entire times table up to nine by nine. Then William Ephraim, who bragged that his dad let him smoke cigars.

All that weekend, Myra paced around the apartment. At first, her mother, Doreen, thought it was a good sign: "See, honey, isn't it true what I've been saying? You'll feel so much better if you get some exercise." But by Sunday afternoon, Doreen said all that circling was making her nauseous and that Myra had better stop. "You're gonna pull a muscle, baby, or make me loony, one or the other, so quit it now, okay?"

Myra went into her own room and walked from the closet to the bed, the bed to the closet. She was terrified William would drop a lit cigar into Strawberry's cage and burn up all her shredded newspaper. When William's mother carried the cage back into the classroom on Monday morning, holding it far away and wrinkling her nose, Myra ran over and lifted the blanket to make sure Strawberry was still alive.

"I let it out and it pooped in my sister's shoe," William told everyone.

"Her name is Strawberry," Myra said quietly. She could tell

194

Strawberry had had a terrible weekend. When you took the guinea pig home, you were supposed to change her newspaper every day, but there were the damp, matted comics from last Thursday. Strawberry had probably meant to poop in William's shoe but made a mistake.

"We're up to the *F*'s Ferris," Mrs. Metcalf said. Myra jumped from her seat, burst toward the front of the room, and almost stumbled over Teddy Bullock's dirty sneaker, stuck like a thumb into the lane between the rows of desks. "Walrus," he hissed.

Myra pressed her arms flat to her sides and watched the floor for feet. She wasn't afraid of tripping, but of stepping on someone by accident, like the last time, when Nina Adamson screamed as if she'd been slapped and told everyone she could see Myra's footprint on her new beige tights.

This time, she made it to Mrs. Metcalf's desk without anything bad happening to anyone.

"Here's the permission slip, dear. Get your mother to sign it, and make sure to save the newspaper all this week."

"I started saving it when we were on the *B*'s," Myra said softly. She had it all planned. On Friday afternoon, she would get a whole seat to herself in the bus. "Strawberry gets upset if strangers are too close to her," she would explain to anyone who tried sitting down. "Once a substitute put her hand in to feed her, and Strawberry bit off the top of her little finger." The other kids would look worried and impressed.

On Saturday, she and Strawberry would get up early and watch *Scooby-Doo,* the guinea pig in Myra's lap, sharing Cap'n Crunch with no milk, the way Myra liked it. Then she'd make a leash from the belt of one of her dresses and take Strawberry on a tour of the apartment complex.

She would change the shredded newspaper every day, as soon as her mother had gone through the TV page and circled her programs, and at night she'd let Strawberry sleep in her bed. She'd be so careful not to roll over and crush her. Myra would stroke the tiny ears, soft as pansies, and scratch Strawberry just behind the head, feeling the silky points of bone underneath. They would fall asleep at the same time. On Monday, they might forget to go back to school.

Myra kept the permission slip in her pocket until after Doreen got home from the dry cleaners, washed the chemical stink out of her hair, and put two new coats of Taffy Apple on her nails. The space around the couch smelled like candied fruit. Doreen watched *Jeopardy* and fluttered her hands in the air.

In the meantime, Myra tried to cook a frozen dinner, but smoke started to curl out of the toaster oven. She was afraid her mother would yell, like the time when she poured hot tea in the glass and it burst into pieces right there on the kitchen counter. So she cut the blue edges off some cheese and ate that, waxy dominoes of it on top of five Ritz crackers.

If Strawberry was here, Myra thought, we could share the crackers and read out loud at the kitchen table. Would Strawberry like a story about other animals? She could read that one the library lady read—she forgot the name of it—about the special pig and the clever rat and the spider who wrote words in her web.

Finally, she tiptoed over to the couch during a commercial and showed the note to Doreen. "What's this, you get in trouble?"

"No, it's about the guinea pig. Strawberry. It's my turn to take her home for the weekend, Nina and Teddy and William already did, but I named her and take the best care of her. I'll clean up she won't bother you at all—I promise. Can I, please?"

"Shh . . . I'll look at it in a minute. Meantime, you need to get your sweet butt in bed."

In the morning, Myra found the note on the kitchen table, Doreen's scrawl across the bottom. "Dear Myra's teacher, I am sorry but Myra canot take the ginny pig home for the weekend. In our familee we are not gud with annimuls." She signed it, "Mrs. Doreen Ferris (Myra's mother)."

The word *gud* didn't look right to Myra, so she closed up the top of the *u* and made it an *o*. Mrs. Metcalf smiled when she read it. "Your mother's right, dear. We are not God with animals. I'm sorry you can't take Strawberry home, but you can play with her here in the classroom." She handed the note back.

At her desk, Myra scribbled black over "Mrs." and "family." She knew why Doreen didn't want her to take Strawberry. It was because of the fish.

When Myra was five, she'd begged and begged for a goldfish. Doreen tried to talk her out of it. "What do you want with a fish? They just swim around and never go anywhere." When Myra kept asking, Doreen sat her down at the kitchen table. "Don't think it'll be more fun around here once you get a fish. You think it'll change your life, having some new live thing in the house, but it won't. I'm just telling you, because I do have a little more experience. So don't come crying to me when you wake up still chubby and nobody calls to invite you to their birthday party and the fish doesn't even give a good goddamn whether you're miserable or happy as long as you give it its little sprinkle of fish food."

"Okay," said Myra. "But can I get one anyway?"

Doreen hustled her down to Woolworth's, and they came home with a round glass bowl and a pet in a plastic bag. The fish was the color of the orange-yellow crayon in Myra's box. She named it Waldo.

A few weeks later, Myra's cousin Jimmy had to sleep over because his mom was sick. Actually, she wasn't sick, just scared. It happened sometimes. Myra always knew because Doreen would get a voice like a cheerleader on the phone, saying, "Come on, Crystal, you just got to get yourself outta that bed, I know you got the gumption in you, girl. . . ." Finally, she would sigh and say, "All right, I'll come on over and fetch him." Then Doreen would crash the phone back into its cradle. "She blew it. She had a chance with that Larry fellow, and that job at the video place, and she blew it. How come I'm the only responsible person in this entire family? Huh? Don't bother answering me." She snapped the door behind her.

Anyway, it was Jimmy's idea to feed cereal to Waldo. At first, Myra said no, he only ate fish food, but Jimmy talked her into just a little bit of Puffa Puffa Rice. She brought the box and he poured. "No, enough," she whispered as Puffa Puffa Rice settled into the bottom of the fish bowl and Waldo swam crazily between the falling grains. Jimmy kept pouring, and after a while, Myra cupped her hands over her face. "Please stop. Please stop. Please," she whispered into the dark shell of her palms.

Later, when the bowl was full of cereal and Waldo was blank and quiet, Doreen scooped him out with a ladle and marched to the bathroom with her jaw locked like a gate that said NO SEC-OND CHANCES. Myra covered her ears, but she heard the flush anyway, a hungry slurp that took Waldo away for good. Doreen hit the handle again, and Myra crawled under the covers of her bed, pulling the blanket so tightly around her face, she could barely breathe.

While Mrs. Metcalf taught how to divide big numbers into little ones, Myra crumpled up the permission slip and stuck it inside her desk. Later, after she'd finished her work sheet, she walked back to Strawberry's cage. The window was open, and the April air felt like warm pajamas. Strawberry was hiding beneath a mound of torn-up car ads.

Myra reached into the cage. "Hey, Strawberry, I saved you something from the cafeteria." The guinea pig waddled out of her nest and sniffed at the carrot stick in Myra's hand. Myra could feel Strawberry's breath, a moist glove around her fingertips. She leaned over the cage and picked up the guinea pig with both hands. Strawberry felt like a fur bag full of Superballs, soft and loose and lumpy.

Myra glanced around; everyone was still bent over their long division. She needed to hold the guinea pig close, closer, so she'd know that Myra would never hurt her, not in a million years, so Myra could explain that she still missed Waldo and was sorry, so sorry, about what had happened.

Myra stretched out the neck of her dress and slipped Strawberry inside. The guinea pig's toenails scrabbled over her collarbone, and she made a few little squeaks. "Shhh . . ." Myra could feel the tiny heart racing against her own. She held Strawberry's head up and whispered to her: "See over there, behind the car lot and the liquor store—that's where I live. I was going to show you all around and read to you and give you crackers that weren't even stale yet, but my stupid mother won't let me."

"Hey, Myra's got the pig. She's got the pig! It's in her dress!" Robbie Tupperman yelled.

Myra jumped, and suddenly Strawberry was on the book-shelf, scuttling toward the open window. There was screaming and hands and Strawberry moving too fast, zigzagging in one direction, then the other, back and forth across the shelf and finally over the sill and out into the frame of blue. Myra felt queasy, as if she herself were falling through slow, sticky space. Her arms and legs twitched, and her face throbbed. Robbie and some other kids climbed up on the windowsill and stuck their heads out.

"There she is, in those sticker bushes," said Cathy Kohl.

"If she's dead, it's all your fault," said Rose-Ellen Murphy.

"It's not anyone's fault," Mrs. Metcalf said. "When creatures are startled, they sometimes try to run. We're not always quick enough to stop them. Myra, why don't you come outside with me? It's just a few feet down. I think Strawberry might be okay."

Myra stayed on the grass while Mrs. Metcalf hiked up her skirt and marched into the sticker bushes under the third-grade win-dows. When she turned around, she had Strawberry in her arms. "From the way she's holding her leg, I think it might be broken. She'll probably have a limp. But it looks like she's going to sur-vive. If cats have nine lives, I guess guinea pigs must have at least three or four. Here." She held out the pig toward Myra.

"No, you hold her," Myra said. Then tears started falling from her eyes, splatting into the dirt. "I—love—Strawberry," she man-aged to hiccup before something salty burst in her throat and filled up her mouth and all her thoughts swam away. She'd had one lucky break, getting to name Strawberry, but it didn't mean anything, because she'd almost killed her. We are not good with animals, she thought. Not good. Myra wrapped her arms tightly around her chest to keep everything from shaking loose.

By high school, Teddy Bullock called her "Walrus" only occasionally, like when she dropped her milk carton on the cafeteria floor or broke the titration pipette during a chemistry lab. The other kids didn't call her anything at all. When the phone rang in the evening, Doreen bounced up from the couch, a smile teasing around her jaw.

"Oh, ho, ho, could be for you this time," she told Myra. "Never answer on the first ring; otherwise, they'll think you're, you know, desperate." Doreen lifted the phone to her ear, drew her "hel-lo-o" out to three expectant syllables. Then her expression sagged when it turned out to be someone selling magazines or cable TV or asking her opinion about the school bond levy.

"Next time," she said, and patted Myra's knee. "You know, sweetheart, anytime you want to go and get one of those makeovers with me, you just say the word." Myra shrugged. She hated the sound of it—makeover. Like that recipe in home ec that turned out all wrong because she left out the baking powder and then she had to stay after school and do it again, alone, until the biscuits puffed up like they were supposed to. Make over. It didn't sound like something that should be done to people.

"I'm going to bed," she said.

"What? It's early." Doreen patted the warm spot on the couch. "Don't you want to watch with me? You gonna leave your momma out here all by her lonesome?" Doreen pouted, her lower lip stuck out, pink as baloney.

"I'm going to bed," Myra repeated.

Eventually, Doreen quit nagging Myra to fix her hair and put on lipstick and for God sake try to lose a little weight. She was distracted; she'd fallen in love with a customer at the cleaner's, a red-haired man named Tyrone who came in every Thursday with two brown suits to be cleaned and pressed. Doreen moved the TV into her room, and Myra could hear her listening to the Monday-night movie and practicing things to say to Tyrone someday. "It feels dangerous to love you so much. . . . You've turned my life around. . . . Oh, Ty, do we deserve to be this happy?"

In her own room, Myra put on a white nightgown with wide bell-shaped sleeves. She moved her arms up and down a few times, watching the fabric billow and float. Then she stood in front of the mirror with her feet apart and her arms stretched—a snow angel, snowflake, the rich, fluffy kind that touches you so lightly, you can't even feel it.

Myra climbed up on her bed and bounced, trying to hit softly as a snowflake that could fall and never make a dent. Then she let herself bounce higher and higher, her feet leaving the mattress and punching down again, the nightgown flapping at her feet, hair stinging her eyes, her voice making little sounds— *"aieyy, aieyy"*—even though she didn't mean to, and then one foot caught in the hem of her nightgown and she slipped off the bedspread, crumpled to the floor, and banged her elbow against the bookcase. A small ceramic cat, a gift from her aunt Crystal, spun off the top shelf and shattered on the linoleum.

"Myra, what the hell are you doing in there?"

"Nothing. Nothing." Myra swept the china pieces into one hand and tried to fit the zigzag points back together. "I didn't mean it," she whispered. She closed her fingers around the broken cat and squeezed until it hurt.

That year, her last in high school, Myra took computer classes, word processing, and was startled to find out she was good at it. The words flew from her hands like flags, as if she had been born knowing that *W* was next to *E* and that quotation marks lay just beneath your stretched-out right-hand pinkie.

At her first job interview after graduation, the boss came out from behind the desk. She wore a black-and-white suit and looked crisp as a new saddle shoe. "You scored higher on the test than any other applicant in the history of Handel and Messinger," she said, and reached her hand toward Myra.

Myra's head filled up with warm Jell-O. "I didn't cheat," she said, then knew from the fever behind her eyes that that was the wrong answer.

"Of course you didn't. All our tests are computer-monitored. Can you begin tomorrow?"

"Yes. In the morning? I mean, of course you would want me to start in the morning. That's when you open, right?" She closed her mouth before any more mistakes could run out, then saw the nameplate, green and gold, on the desk and thought she ought to add, "Mrs. Franklin."

The boss smiled with her perfect teeth. "It's Ms. But please call me Eleanor."

Myra typed and filed, sent invoices, organized bulk mailings by zip code. She liked the way paper chattered out of the computer printer, all the type sharp and even. She was careful with the machines, the purring gray computer and the fax with its two blinking green eyes. Once, a letter disappeared into the Xerox machine and didn't come back; Eleanor walked by just as Myra was crouching down to pull the stained sheet out of the rollers. She stood up and wiped streaks of toner onto her dress. "Look what—I mean, I must have done something. . . . I'm sorry—did I break it?"

"Nah, happens all the time. At least you managed to get the damn thing out. Last time, it completely shredded a letter, just gobbled it for lunch, and we had to call the repairman." Eleanor gave the machine a friendly little kick, and Myra flinched. Wasn't she afraid of hurting it?

At lunchtime, when the other secretaries walked in a laughing cluster to the Brown Bag Luncheonette, Myra went to Mr. Weinberg's pet store on Seventh Avenue. She watched the dogs show off in their cages, and the cats, which pretended they didn't care but really wanted someone to notice how well they'd licked their fur down flat. There was a parakeet that whistled "You're the Top," and a pair of toast brown rabbits, and tank after tank of fish. A clerk named Lucy, who had pink hair and an earring in her nose, fed the animals and cleaned their cages.

"You're sure in here a lot. You got something—a cat or a dog— at home?" Lucy asked one afternoon. Myra shook her head.

"You must be allergic. Too bad. My dad, he's so allergic, his eyes swell up and he breaks out in hives if he even goes in a room where a cat's been. It figures. I think allergies are caused by bad karma, you know, like if you were a hypocrite in a former life, you sneeze whenever you get near a dog. Cause animals are like babies—they can tell in a second if you're not for real. They know things."

"Really?" Myra said.

"Oh, totally. Now that parakeet, Fritz, the one who whistles Cole Porter—remember the night the store got robbed? Well, right before it happened, when that creep was still acting like he was all into the snakes, asking me a million questions while his buddy stuck up Mr. Weinberg—well, Fritz wouldn't shut up. And then last month, when Mr. Weinberg's wife had a stroke and he missed two weeks of work, it was like all the animals knew. They got real quiet and sad and didn't eat very much."

"That's very interesting," Myra said.

"Yeah, well, it's the truth. I know for a fact these creatures are smarter than my parents. Sure you don't want to hold one?" And she held out a fluffy tea-colored cat.

"I'm sure. I've got to get back to work. They don't like it when I'm late." Myra tried to get back from lunch before the other secretaries. She hated to ride the elevator upstairs with them, mashed together all the way to the eleventh floor, trying not to poke people with her elbow or breathe too hard on their hair. The women's talk was loose and careless—books and department store sales, restaurants and boyfriends and movies—and Myra felt awkward and silent and huge. So it was better, for everyone really, if she cut her lunches five minutes short and rode the elevator alone.

In January, Weinberg's and the travel agency down the street sponsored a contest. You had to guess how many babies would be born in the store by the first day of spring, and that included new fish, kittens, puppies, rabbits, lizards, everything. For weeks, Myra walked from cage to cage, looking at the thick-bellied mother cats and dogs. She peered closely at the swollen fish. The striped rabbit. The gecko with two pearly eggs in her translucent belly. She calculated quietly. On the last day of the contest, Myra wrote her name, address, and phone number on the pink slip of paper by the fishbowl, and in the space that said, "Guess the babies———" she printed carefully, "Forty-seven."

The prize for the third-closest guess was a round glass aquarium, along with any fish in the store. Myra hoped she wouldn't win that. The second-closest would get a new puppy, winner's choice. Myra imagined all the terrible things that might happen to her puppy. She might forget to feed it, and come home to find it shaking from starvation in the corner. It might strangle itself in the cord from the venetian blinds. It might run into the street and be squashed by a taxicab. Myra pictured herself falling to her knees by the curb, lifting her dress to make a hammock for the bleeding puppy, her face steaming with tears.

The grand prize, for the person who guessed exactly right, was two nights in Key West. Myra found it on the map, a tiny wart that fell off the finger of Florida. She imagined a heavy wooden key unlocking a small red door, like in *Alice in Wonderland*. She could eat the cake that said "eat me" and wait to see what she turned into.

Then she got it. The whole day was confusing—first, Mr. Weinberg on the phone, saying, "You won, Myra, my girl. Mazel tov!" She could hear the new puppies in the background, whimpering, "Are you, are you, are you," and the kittens' thin whine: "Me now, me now." Then a travel agent with a sugary voice called her to talk about poolside views and aisle seats and sweethearts.

"What?" Myra said.

"Well, the package is for two. Don't you want to take that special someone?"

"I don't have a special someone," she told the sugary voice.

"Well, all righty, then, maybe this will be your opportunity to meet Mr. Right. Could be the chance of a lifetime. I'll just reserve one seat, then? No smoking? Can I have your last name? I'll just mail out these tickets, then. All righty."

Doreen said it had to be a scam. "You be careful now, they don't stick you with a big bill when it's all over. That's how those things work, you know. Think you're taking a free ride, then find out it costs."

She stood in the doorway and smoked while Myra folded T-shirts and a bathing suit into a suitcase. The sunscreen gel the lady at the drugstore recommended. A windbreaker because the girls at work said it could get cool at night. A mystery novel someone lent her, with blood drops coming off the words on the cover. She snapped the suitcase and sat down beside it on the bed.

"This'll be the first night we ever spent apart," Doreen said.

"I know it."

"I remember the first night I had you, still laid up in the hospital, couldn't even pee without that burning from the stitches, but there you were, eyes all scrunched up like a bud that hasn't opened yet, and I felt sorta like God must've felt, you know, when he made all the birds and trees, thinking, I did something good." She snorted. "Huh. Then the next day I brought you home and found they'd repo'd the car while I was in the hospital.

"That was some time," she said. "You so little, and me not even twenty-one, scared I was going to mess up at this mom business. One day, I just left you there yelling in your crib, went out and walked around the whole block. I think I was half-hoping the child welfare would come and take you while I was gone, and half-scared I'd have to go back and be in charge."

She handed Myra a small packet wrapped in the TV page. "Here. Open it after the plane takes off. You go have yourself a good time."

She left the room, then stuck her head back in. "But not too good. If you know what I mean."

Myra had no idea. "Okay. Okay," she said.

The man with the white hair and the earring—he was one of the two who owned the bed-and-breakfast—wanted to know if Myra would be needing snorkel equipment. It was complimentary.

"What?" Myra said.

"Will you be wanting to snorkel? There's a reef. We recommend it to all our guests. You'll want to go early, before the mobs descend."

"Oh . . . well, okay. I've never been snorkeling, but I know how to swim. They made us take a test at school to pass our PE credit; we had to swim all the way across—I'm sorry, I talk too much. I guess you probably get tired of listening to people all day."

"Not at all. I'm Antoine, by the way." He leaned forward as if sharing a secret. His skin smelled spicy. "I *despised* PE class. All those kids with their muddy sneakers, ruining the best dance floor in the school. You know what I used to tell the teacher?"

Myra shook her head.

"That it was my time of the month." Antoine hooted and slapped his head. "I was so baaaddd." His laugh was like those colored gum balls coming out of the little metal gate in the machine, dropping right into your hand. Myra laughed with him.

"I'll bring the snorkel gear to your door. Let me know if there's anything else you need. By the way, that shade of green— actually, I suppose it's teal—is just smashing on you."

Myra looked down at her bathing suit. Teal. Sounded like something you could taste, a smooth drink, the ice cool and crunchy, with a leaf floating in the glass. "I didn't know it was teal," she said. "But I'm glad."

"Good," Antoine said. "Excellent."

Myra found the package from her mother in the side pocket of her suitcase. It was a twelve-pack of condoms and a note that said, "You can't be to carfull. Luv, Doreen." Then the "Doreen" was scribbled over, and "Mom" written underneath it. Myra stuck the condoms in the drawer of the night table.

The next morning, she walked down to the beach, carrying the snorkel gear. The rubber flippers were twice as long as her feet, and the strap of the mask hurt where it mashed her ears flat against her head. She saw other snorkelers walk into the water backward, so they wouldn't trip over their feet. Myra found a place where she wouldn't be in anyone's way, and she imitated the others, placing her heels carefully on the soft, shifting ground.

The first wave smacked her on the rear end, cold, like sitting on a metal chair. Myra stuck the snorkel tube in her mouth and practiced breathing the way Antoine had said, making a *tuh* sound with the exhale to clear water from the tube. Waves nudged her back and forth. The ocean was green—no, teal—and lacy where it hit the sand. Myra put her head down and started paddling. Breathing out—*tuh*—then sucking air in. *Tuh. Whihh-hhh. Tuh. Whihhhhh.* She waggled her feet and pushed forward through the soft green.

A blur of silver winked by, then circled back to shimmy in front of her. The fish's color changed in the light like those little magic squares on credit cards—blue, then gray, then silver, then black. Planks of sun leaning into the water like in Bible pictures, the fish dancing back and forth. Then suddenly, something stopped working; she was breathing wet and coughing salt, tears in her eyes and her throat tight and hot, frantic to get out of the mask, sputtering up into the blue sky with her feet skidding over the ocean floor.

Myra stood up and coughed brine out of her throat. There was sand in her flippers, water in her mask. She'd seen one fish, and it was beautiful; maybe that was enough. She squinted across the sand; Antoine was hammering new trim to the veranda overhang. He leaned off his ladder and waved. Water sucked at her legs, the warmth pulling her down, down. The gripped feeling in her throat relaxed until she could breathe without gasping. She wanted to go under again, down where everything was pudding-soft and window-clear, where her body was silk and her move-ments in slow motion, down where nothing could break and no one would die.

She waved back to Antoine, then crouched, letting the ocean seal itself around her. *Tuh. Whihhhh.* Fish zigzagged toward her, then away. There was a tubby black one with white dots, one with a long snout like a pencil, one that looked tie-dyed, blue and orange and red. They swam right up to her face. They were not afraid of her big white arms or floppy rubber feet. She followed the pencil-nose fish until it vanished under a ridge of coral. She watched the pretty tie-dye fish chase a tiny yellow one.

Myra thought about Waldo drowning in Puffa Puffa Rice, and Strawberry landing on her feet in the sticker bushes. Just because you named something didn't mean you had to be in charge of it forever. The fish flirted up close, the fish darted away, and Myra swam with them, beside them, breathing under water like God's own miracle, each *tuh* a firm push of her tongue, each clear col-umn of air another chance.

I Seen Some Stuf Horabl Stuf Lisen

Avi asked me the other day if God has a last name. We were on Lincoln Drive, the curvy part, where the speed-limit sign says 25, so everyone slows down to forty. He was in back, in his car seat. It's not like those infant or toddler car seats, hard plastic cocoons with padded insides; this one is more like a booster chair in a restaurant. Avi graduated to it last month when he turned six. He's small for his age.

We had a ritual for saying good-bye to the old car seat. First, we looked at it together and Avi told me stories. "Mom, see that orange spot? That's from the time I threw up after those French fries, remember?" I remembered. "And here's where I crayoned on it. I was little then." He says this with breezy confidence. He does not regret the past or punish himself for being young. Maybe that is the difference between children and adults.

We scrubbed the old car seat the best we could, tied a purple ribbon to the strap, and walked it around the corner to Michael and Amy's house. "Hi, this is for Mira," Avi said when Michael answered the bell. He had that new-parent glaze in his eyes, and slightly delayed reactions to everything. He looked at us through the screen for about thirty seconds before he remembered to open the door. They only got back from India with Mira a couple of weeks ago, and Michael said her clock was all mixed up; she slept all day and screamed all night. Also, she vomited formula across the room. I told him to try the soy stuff, that lots of dark-skinned kids are allergic to cow's milk. Anyway, Amy and Mira were both asleep, so we set the car seat down in the living room and walked home.

"You know what God told me in my dream?" Avi said.

"Nope. What?"

"God told me Mira's going to be my friend when she grows up."

"Really? That's great, Av. She'll be a lucky kid, to have you as a friend."

He talks about God a lot lately: What does God wear? Who are God's friends? Is the God in Benita's church the same as the one at our synagogue?

And then, in the car, on the part of Lincoln Drive that most provokes me to hasty, whispered prayer: "Does God have a last name?"

"I don't think so, Av. Just one name. Like Cher."

I could feel my pious great-uncle, Avi Morgenstein, the one for whom I named Avi, scowling at my lack of reverence. Yeah, for you it was easy to believe, I thought. You davened every morning, you went to the shoe factory, at noon you came home and Tanta Flora gave you a little schmaltz on rye bread. Your God gave clear commandments, and you obeyed: You never wrote on Shabbes; you killed your chickens with one swift slash to the throat; you never coveted Mrs. Seligman next door.

But me, Uncle Avi, I don't live by the Big Ten, and nobody has a brisket waiting when I get home from the office. It's a lot harder, since Nancy left, to figure out what's sure—let alone answer Avi's questions about the woman with the plastic hat outside the 7-Eleven, or the blown-up buildings on the news, or God. I joined a shul, mostly for the company and so Avi could hang out with other Jewish kids, but I've never been much of a believer—in love at first sight, in the power of positive thinking, in "till death do us part." One thing I like about Judaism, though, is this business about atonement—the idea that you can use your words and actions to try to patch up the past. I've been trying to explain it to Avi, in kid terms, of course, and I think he's getting it, though he keeps mixing up the words *apologize* and *forgive*.

Someone told me, when I was pregnant with Avi, that if I didn't believe in God before I went into labor, I would when it was done. But childbirth, amazing as it was, didn't make a disciple out of me. Actually, it confirmed my faith in chaos. Out of that syringeful of yellowish gunk and a pinprick egg floating somewhere inside me, out of all that blood and pain and screaming came a shiny, wet package, a crimped-up chimpanzee, my perfect son. Who has my crooked nose, my mother's bottle green eyes, true Morgenstein feet with wide, splayed toes—and the cinnamon skin and tight-coiled hair of donor number 612 from the Sperm Bank of California.

Nancy and I had done all the research, processed until we were blue. We picked an African-American donor so the kid might look a bit like both of us. When Avi started, around age three, to notice that some families had a big guy who wore Jockey shorts and we didn't, we had our answer ready: "That's right, we don't have a dad. We have a mom, and a Nancy, and an Avi."

He took that as one more truth of existence, with about the same level of importance he gave to the fact that we had a Toyota, while Benita's family drove a Chevy van, or that we ate cheeseburgers at home but not at Sam's house because Sam's Bubbe kept kosher. Once in the supermarket checkout line, he started singing, "We don't have a Da-ad, we don't have a Da-ad."

"Hey, that's cool, buddy," said the checkout clerk. He looked about seventeen and had a silver stud in his eyebrow. "I haven't seen my old man since I was six, and look how great I turned out." He reached across the conveyor belt and gave Avi a high-five. I tried to imagine my son with a pierced brow, a job, his own money. I wondered how the checkout clerk's mom had managed in the years since the old man left.

Nancy was the one who really wanted a kid. I was pretty content with the way things were: my job with the literacy program, my tulips, volunteering once a month with Habitat for Humanity, sipping Negro Modelo on the porch of our stamp-sized row house. But Nan was so persuasive about it—how a kid would stretch us, make us better people, and how much fun it would be—that I finally said yes, and I even agreed to be the one who got pregnant, because I was four years younger.

I was lucky; it took on the second try, and as soon as we saw the pink line on the home pregnancy test, Nancy went a little crazy, started buying packages of onesies, which looked like white cotton burrito wraps, and terry-cloth socks that barely fit my big toe, and a million books on labor, nursing, child rearing. Despite the pink line, I wasn't really convinced I was pregnant until the fourth month, when I couldn't zip my favorite skirt, not even lying on the bed with my stomach sucked in. Like I said, I'm not much of a believer.

I came home from the hospital cranky and exhausted, and I stayed that way for about three months. Sometimes when Avi cried at night, I'd put the pillow over my head and kvetch to Nan, "Those goddamn cats," and she'd have to remind me it was no cat, it was our kid, and I was the one with the breast milk, remember? Avi lost the hair he had at birth and started looking like a miniature suntanned Yoda, with his serious wrinkled brow. As if he were taking inventory of my parenting skills and finding me sorely lacking in critical areas like patience and lullabies.

Nancy could rock for hours, creaking the chair back and forth, singing Broadway show tunes. She put Avi to sleep with the score from *My Fair Lady*. As soon as we convinced him that a bottle was almost as good as my raw, overworked nipples, Nancy took over the 4:00 A.M. feeding. She bought all the Newbery Medal books and could go through *Goodnight Moon* twelve times in a row, while I was more apt to cheat and read Avi, in my sweetest, most calming voice, Maureen Dowd's latest op-ed in the *New York Times*.

I couldn't stand most of the children's books, with their singsongy rhymes and saccharine endings. Even the supposedly PC ones, with cheerful multicultural families and two dads and single moms, still seemed more than I could live up to. The parents in those books never served broccoli and string cheese for dinner because they were too exhausted to think of anything else; they never took their kid to Rite Aid at two in the morning because at least it was air-conditioned. And they never screamed at their partner, on a muggy October Tuesday, "What do you mean you'll be home late again? I've been here all day changing diapers, and you were the one who wanted this kid in the first place!" then punched the phone back into its cradle. That afternoon, I ran upstairs to see if Avi had managed to nap through the noise. He had, thank God.

But I know he was awake, listening from under his rainbow comforter, on other nights, when Nancy and I sat stalemated at the dining room table, spitting bitter crumbs at each other. She was home less and less, full of careful explanations about project deadlines, new commissions for fussy clients, subcontractors who needed to be watched like hawks.

"I didn't sign up to do this by myself," I hissed one night.

"You didn't sign anything," she said. "Neither did I."

I should have picked up the clues: Nancy got avid when there was something—or someone—new to be avid about. She was great at beginnings. When we first met, she courted me with a dozen helium balloons delivered to the office on my birthday, a full-body massage if I complained about a crick in my neck. But Avi wasn't a beginning anymore. He'd grown a tiny fuzzy Afro, talked in full sentences, expressed strong opinions about sandboxes (he approved) and baths (he didn't). Had favorite colors—purple one week, the next a shade he called "suncloud"—and foods (nix on cantaloupe, yay on mushrooms). He was a kid, a lifetime unscrolling in front of us, and I could feel Nancy pulling away.

I did desperate things, things I have yet to atone for. I looked in her wallet. I picked up the receiver oh so quietly when she took late-night calls in her study. I stopped buying the kind of coffee she liked and said I just forgot. Once I pitched her favorite mug across the kitchen. It hit the stove and cracked into toothy pieces. Avi watched the whole thing.

"Why you do that?" he said.

"It was an accident." Later, I wanted to throw myself on my

knees and beg forgiveness. Not from God—from my son, who surely, at the age of three, knew the difference between a cup that slips out of your hand and one that is flung across the room, who knew the difference between a mortifying truth and a pathetic lie.

The clues I sleuthed out added up to the conclusion I suspected, and while that didn't excuse my violations, it did give me a reason to ask Nancy to get the hell out. She was packed and gone in two days, leaving me to explain our topsy-turvy world.

"Mommy and Nancy had some big fights," I began, Avi on my lap. "Maybe you heard us yelling. We were very mad, and sometimes when grown-ups are very mad and they can't make up, it's better if they don't live in the same house anymore. You can visit Nancy sometimes, on weekends. Do you have questions about that?"

"Who's going to read to me?" he said.

"Well, I will." A little defensive. Thinking, You're stuck, kid. I got you, and you got the parent who can't sing and hates Disney movies and doesn't even believe in God. Sure sucks the way things work out, doesn't it?

But that wasn't the worst. A few months later, we were at the supermarket, I was rushing to get our groceries paid for and us home in time to feed and bathe Avi and get him to bed before a bunch of people came over to talk about the neighborhood watch program. Avi started singing, "We don't have a Nan-cy, we don't have a Nan-cy." And grief and fury, all those nights of avoiding the cold side of the bed, boiled up, splashed out in a direct line to my hand, and I slapped Avi once, smartly, on his cheek. He purpled with shock and fear, and held his breath, like he used to do as a baby. But unlike then, when he'd finally cut loose with a gulp and a howl, this time he just let the air slowly out of his clenched mouth. The clerk with the eyebrow ring clutched my last bag of groceries and stared at me.

"What?" I said fiercely, grabbed the sack, and shoved two twenties at him. "Keep the change."

Avi didn't say a word as I tossed groceries in the trunk, buckled him into the car seat and got behind the steering wheel. I kept glancing into the rearview mirror, but he was staring out the window. I wanted to hurt myself, except my chest already felt like I'd had open-heart surgery. I'd severed something between us, an artery, an umbilical. Always, my kid would remember: the day Mom hit me at the Acme.

And then I ran over a bird. Not a big one—a baby, maybe just learning to fly. I couldn't swerve fast enough. I saw it wobble into view, hit the grille, then the sickening *thuk-thuk* as the front, then rear tires went over it. Avi seemed not to notice. But I felt something rip behind my breastbone, and the whole sac of sorrow came pouring out. I was sobbing, deep, choking sobs that swept out the bottoms of my lungs, came up in wet, snotty clumps. I pulled over, leaned against the steering wheel, and wept for everything broken in my path. Finally, I managed to get us home and park the car in front of the house. I crawled over the front seat and curled up beside Avi. I unbuckled his seat belt and lifted him into my lap.

"Avi, that was an awful thing I did. I was angry and sad, but that's no reason to hit someone. I'm so sorry, sweetheart, I'm just so sorry." I was blubbering. I held Avi for a long time, until my breathing settled down to match his own even, shallow breaths.

"It's okay, Mommy. I apologize you."

An aftershock of tears rose, quivered, subsided. I do not deserve this gift, this bottomless faith.

"Okay, kiddo. I forgive."

I've never hit Avi again. At least not so far. After a year, I could finally stand to read the parenting books Nancy left behind. And now that Avi's old enough to appreciate *Winnie-the-Pooh,* we've found some common ground. I still worry that I've scarred him, with my temper and my lies, that I've already torn the delicate fabric of trust and belief, and that I may do worse. I worry that Nancy's leaving was really my fault, that if I'd been a more devout partner, more of a believer, she'd have stayed.

Avi doesn't let me stay still, ruminating; he is always pointed forward. We have our best conversations when we are in the car, covering ground.

"Mom, when will I be old enough to not take naps?"

I give a wild, hopeful guess: "How 'bout when you're ten?"

"Nah, that's old. I'm gonna be an architect by then. That's what Nancy is, right?"

"Yep," I said. "Hey, kiddo, what interesting stuff happened at school today?" I've learned from the books that if you ask a kid, "What did you do in school?" chances are he'll say, "Nothing," so you have to ask another way.

"We wrote stories. A special teacher came in."

"Oh, yeah? What was she like?"

"She was funny. She wore a hat. She asked us about a time when we got scared, and then she helped us write it down."

My stomach rolled. Great. Next week, I'd probably be getting phone calls from Child Protective Services, asking about the supermarket incident, telling me my son has nightmares about broken crockery.

"What did you write about?"

"I don't know. Stuff." Then he started drumming, a reggae tempo, on the back of my seat. That's a clear conversation ender, I don't care what the books say. But later that night, when I was going through his backpack to get rid of the uneaten peanut butter sandwich—I keep forgetting he doesn't like it anymore—I found the story. It was called, "I Seen Some Stuf Horabl Stuf Lisen." I felt queasy. I had to sit down.

"I seen a smashed bird in the street it flew into a car," he wrote. So much for staring out the window. "I seen on TV a boy tooked a gun to school and shoot and shoot. I seen some kids break my mom's tulips and throw them." Damn. And I'd been so careful about laying blame, deciding it was wild rabbits who'd wreaked havoc on my flower bed.

"I seen my mom"—and I had to stop there, get a glass of water, and sit back down—"I seen my mom be sad she crying on the porch."

That was all. At the bottom he wrote, in all-capital letters, "Avi Morgenstein-Parsons," the hyphenated name he still carries, emblem of joining and brokenness, faith and loss, the fragile little dash a bridge he'll have to cross on his own. I smoothed out the wrinkles in his story and read it again.

"Mom?"

I went to him, still sniffling.

"You sad?"

"Uh-huh. Sometimes things just make me cry."

"Me, too. Hey, Mom?"

"Yeah?"

"Knock, knock."

"Who's there?"

"Me!" he yelped, and stood up in bed in his Superman pajamas. I hugged him, wetting his waist with tears.

"Okay," I said. "Me, too."

Diamonds Are a Girl's Best Friend

Vannie was sure she had broken something. A rib, maybe, or some important and unfixable bone crouched near her heart. Everything in her chest shimmied for a second, and she felt bundled in static, like the cackle of the television between stations. Finally, a clear phrase punched through: Someone was yelling, "Run! Vannie, run!" and she let the bat drop to the plate and went.

She'd never hit the ball before. Not in a real game, the kind with uniforms and lemonade and the stands filled up with dads in sandals and mothers with sunblock. The truth was, she hadn't been trying that hard. The Owls were ahead by four runs, it was the bottom of the sixth inning, and pearls of sweat kept rolling under Vannie's collar as she waited on the bench for her turn. Actually, she'd been trying to recall the formula for figuring the circumference of a circle. Pi times something. And what was pi, anyway, little cuneiform of sticks, like a kindergartener's drawing of a house: two walls, roof slapped on top, flimsy enough to blow over with a sneeze.

The girl playing first base stood with her fists on her hips, bored and righteous, the posture of a teenager waiting for the parent who is always late for car pool. Girls with older sisters stood like that, a pose that looked just right at fifteen but at twelve, Vannie's age, seemed garish as cherry lipstick. First base. First grade, first aid, first lady. Why did they call the president's wife the first lady, like there might be another one hanging around somewhere in the wings? Firstborn. That was Vannie, not as if she could forget, carrying around her four-syllable truck of a name, Evangeline, after the French-Canadian great-grandmother who took a train across the continent alone at a time when, the relatives always made sure to add, "women just didn't do that."

The other thing the relatives always mentioned about Evangeline was that she kept a small oil painting of her Quebec cottage, the one by the lake where she'd grown up, on the wall in her San Francisco bedroom. It was the first thing she saw in the morning, the last thing she looked at each night before crawling under the eiderdown with her feet, as always, pointing east.

In photographs, the first Evangeline was tall and ivory-colored, stiff as a baseball bat in her gardening apron, with a pinched face and long fingers. She looked as though she wasn't quite acquainted with her own body. It was hard for Vannie to imagine her doing anything regular, like burping or brushing her teeth. Evangeline was twenty, a widow and a mother already, when she put 4,157 miles of North America between her old life and her new one. Vannie wondered what she thought about while that train grumbled through backyards and cornfields on the way to the Pacific Ocean. Did homesick mean sick for home or sick *of* home? Did leaving make it better?

Vannie tapped a sneaker toe on the first-base pad and kept

running. The outfielders dangled their gloves, eyes on the sky, as if they were tracking a flyaway balloon. How far had she hit the ball, anyway? "Go, Vannie, keep running!" someone yelled, and she lit out for second. Just last week, Misty Rosenberg had whispered the other meaning of second base to Vannie in the girls locker room.

"It's when you let the guy feel you up," Misty said.

"Feel you up where?"

"Your tits, dummy. Under your shirt. But not on the first date—otherwise, you'll get a reputation."

Vannie tried to imagine strange hands—Tommy Lafair's, for instance—touching the small mounds of her breasts. How would that work, exactly—would he ask first or just grab at her sweater? Her body was such strange territory lately, with its smells and oiliness, bumps and clockwork ache. No one had told her periods would be so messy, or about the growing meadows of hair inside her thighs. It was like waking up every morning in a different house, tiptoeing around for the first few hours until she got her bearings.

"Why would a guy want to do that?" she asked, thinking of the absent way Tommy Lafair handled his math book, his Frisbee.

"Beats me," Misty said. "They just do."

Vannie rounded second base. Where was the ball? Her teammates were standing up on the bench, pumping their arms and waving as if they could help push her around the diamond by making a breeze. The girl on third base looked sad, shaking her blond braids back and forth. Ninety feet from second to third, from third to home plate. Vannie couldn't remember how she knew that—or the other facts that sometimes popped into her head. The French for room—*la salle*—even before Mr. Bonneau handed out the new vocabulary list. The way to cut flowers, a clean diagonal scissor above the joint in the stem, so they would live longer in a vase.

Or the way to climb out her third-floor bedroom window, fingers curled around the brick sill, and edge along the second-story porch roof before slithering down the drainpipe to the driveway. The house and her body working gently together, as if the bricks had been waiting these twelve years to let her discover a careful, quiet route of escape.

It was last Sunday, a banana moon, and she'd stood in the driveway in her pajamas, looking at the slack curtains, the TV's mercury flicker from her parents' room, and feeling sad. It was so easy, already, to put herself outside the house, to imagine the distance growing and growing and the way she would comfort herself years from now by recalling this exact night: graham cracker of light on the third floor, bruise of blue hydrangeas on the ground.

"Home!" someone screamed. "It's a homer. All right, Vannie! Go for it!" There it was, the batter's cage an open hand and the catcher crouched like a beetle behind the plate, and Vannie sped up, stretching each leg out to capture the next step, kicking dirt and pebbles under her heels. Home, a dusty white polygon peaked at the top like a house roof, and the catcher waiting to catch and the crowd yelling, "Slide, Vannie, SLIDE!"

She'd never slid before, but she knew somehow, knew to fix her eye on the plate, the panting, eager catcher, how to stretch herself along the ground and arrive in a stripe of dust and shadow, and how it would always be like this, circuits of flight and return, the welcome clamorous and confusing, gravel under the skin, feeling as though she'd been gone minutes and eons, and the sting of recognition as she crossed the threshhold, just in time.